Would it all come down to this—their lust exploding on the eighteenth hole?

"So you aim out there?" Autumn squinted into the darkness. "Too bad we don't have a club and some balls...."

"We can't see where we hit." Mike stepped closer, enough that she could feel the heat of his body.

"So what? Just let it fly." Out here under the wide star-scattered sky she felt so free. Anything seemed possible. "I bet I could hit a hole in one in the dark."

"You know what? I just bet you could."

The breeze lifted her hair, snagging a strand on her lip.

He brushed it away with gentle fingers, taking care of her the way he took care of the town and his brother. She felt the sensation of his touch for long seconds. His diamond-chocolate eyes glittered at her, wanting her. He tilted his face, leaned in. He wanted to kiss her.

And she wanted more than just his kiss....

Blaze™

Dear Reader,

For the second book in the DOING IT...BETTER! series about three friends falling in love at thirty-five, I was delighted to haul sexy stripper Autumn Beshkin kicking and screaming to tiny Copper Corners, the sleepy Arizona town I've written about in previous books.

What is it about small towns? I've always lived in cities, but as a child I loved visiting the little burgs in southern Oregon and Idaho where my parents grew up. They had mixed feelings about the lack of privacy and options, but I thought it way cool that everywhere I went—stores, parks, the public pool—people knew me and had a kind word for my folks. Of course, I had nothing to hide and I sure wasn't a stripper secretly sleeping with the mayor!

Which brings me to the point of this story: being valued for all of who you are. Like Autumn, I have always longed to be appreciated for everything about me—my warts and weaknesses as well as my charms and triumphs. Of course, the secret was to value myself. Duh. It's a lesson we all learn and I was happy to help Autumn get there through Mike.

I hope you enjoy Autumn and Mike, who managed to give off a Fourth of July's worth of sparks in this story. Check out www.dawnatkins.com for more about the last book in this three-part series, *At His Fingertips*, out this April! I'd love to hear from you.

Dawn Atkins

AT HER BECK AND CALL

Dawn Atkins

TORONTO • NEW YORK • LONDON
AMSTERDAM • PARIS • SYDNEY • HAMBURG
STOCKHOLM • ATHENS • TOKYO • MILAN • MADRID
PRAGUE • WARSAW • BUDAPEST • AUCKLAND

ISBN-13: 978-0-373-79310-5
ISBN-10:   0-373-79310-3

AT HER BECK AND CALL

ABOUT THE AUTHOR

Dawn Atkins started her writing career in the second grade crafting stories that included every single spelling word her teacher gave her. Since then, she's expanded her vocabulary and her publishing credits. This book is her seventeenth published book. She won the 2005 Golden Quill for Best Sexy Romance and has been a *Romantic Times BOOKreviews* Reviewers Choice finalist for Best Flipside (2005) and Best Blaze (2006). She lives in Arizona with her husband, teenage son and a cat who keeps insisting Dawn give cats' key parts in her books. She, like Autumn and her friends Sugar and Esmeralda, loves prickly pear margaritas and wishes she could live in a town as sweet as Copper Corners. She'd definitely be on the "Autumn Beshkin for Mayor" Committee.

Books by Dawn Atkins

HARLEQUIN BLAZE
93—FRIENDLY PERSUASION
155—VERY TRULY SEXY
176—GOING TO EXTREMES
205—SIMPLY SEX
214—TEASE ME
253—DON'T TEMPT ME...*
294—WITH HIS TOUCH†

HARLEQUIN FLIPSIDE
11—A PERFECT LIFE?

HARLEQUIN DUETS
77—ANCHOR THAT MAN!
91—WEDDING FOR ONE
    TATTOO FOR TWO

HARLEQUIN TEMPTATION
571—THE COWBOY FLING
895—LIPSTICK ON HIS COLLAR
945—ROOM...BUT NOT BORED!
990—WILDE FOR YOU

*Forbidden Fantasies
†Doing It...Better!

To my sister, Wendy Harling,
for her courage...and for being such a fan

1

IT WAS A MEASLY internship in a Podunk town, but Autumn Beshkin was dressed to kill for her interview. One thing you learned cold as a stripper: Appearance counts.

She wore a designer suit and pricey pumps, though the look at the Copper Corners town hall seemed to be casual. And not Friday casual, either. Saturday-washing-the-car casual, judging from Evelyn, the fiftyish secretary who'd ushered her to the folding chair outside the mayor's office. Evelyn wore a tracksuit, ball cap and running shoes.

The phone rang. "H-e-double toothpicks!" Evelyn exclaimed, dropping her fluorescent green knitting to grab it. The fat tabby lolling in her in-box gave an irritated meow, whipping its tail through the loose paperclips on her desk.

"Mayor's office." Evelyn tucked the phone against her ear and clicked her needles into gear again. "Heidi. Oh, yes, your friend's here." Evelyn smiled Autumn's way.

Autumn wiggled her fingers in greeting. Heidi had convinced Autumn to take this job to help Heidi's brother, the mayor, who was "desperate, just *desperate*" for help, since his accountant was on an early maternity leave.

Autumn needed an internship anyway and she'd be

able to room with her best friend and fellow stripper, Jasmine Ravelli, who already had a job here costuming the Founder's Day pageant, so it seemed workable.

"Sure you can talk to him," Evelyn said into the phone. "Hang on a blip." She pushed buttons, then announced, "Mayor Mike, your sister's on line one."

Through the thin paneling behind her head, Autumn heard the mayor greet Heidi. She listened for him to express his gratitude to her for sending Autumn to his rescue.

Instead, he said, "How could you promise her, Heidi? I need a professional, not a college kid."

Autumn sucked in a shocked breath.

"I don't care how mature she is," he continued. "I need someone who knows a P-and-L from the A & P. I don't have time to explain basic procedures. Hell, I don't *know* basic procedures…."

What the…? Not only was the mayor not grateful, he was bitching about her. Autumn's cheeks heated, which made her feel weak. She hated feeling weak.

Already, going back to school at age thirty-four had stirred up the mud at the bottom of her self-esteem pond, mucking up the water with doubts and fears.

Autumn felt competing impulses. *Screw this lame-ass job in this jerkwater town,* followed swiftly by, *If I don't get this lame-ass job in this jerkwater town, I'll just die.* Not quite, but it would throw off her entire program, which she couldn't stand.

"I know she's desperate," the mayor said. "Has to have an internship, yeah, right. Got it. Huh? I'll talk to her, but I don't see how it'll work. What? Hello?"

His muttered "Damn" told Autumn that Heidi had hung up.

The man thought Autumn was desperate? So not fair. *He* was the desperate one.

With her grades, Autumn could easily have scored an internship with a prominent Phoenix accounting firm like the rest of her classmates, but she'd decided this job would offer a broader range of duties. At the big places, she'd be competing with tons of interns and was as likely to get clerical work as quality accounting experience. This had seemed the better choice.

"I'm sure he'll be right with you," Evelyn said to Autumn, smiling reassuringly. She'd evidently read Autumn's alarm as impatience.

"No problem." She managed a faint smile. She had to get this rinky-dink job. All the Phoenix slots had been filled in early June and it was already the nineteenth.

Her eye fell on the motivational quotes sticking out from Evelyn's monitor on a knitted border: *Winners Never Quit...Hang In There...Fake It Till You Make It....*

They all seemed aimed at her. Autumn repeated them in her head, picturing a tiny cheerleading squad shouting out the phrases with a swish of pom-poms. If only she were as sure of herself in her new career as she was as a stripper.

She was doing well in school so far. Her straight A's were the golden treasure she opened in her mind whenever she got scared.

She poked a loose strand of hair into the French braid she'd put her hair in and re-crossed her legs. Her stockings rasped and her garters dug into her thigh. One of the cats where she and Jasmine were house-sitting had snagged her pricey panty hose, so she'd worn the stockings from her Leather Girl dance costume.

Autumn had felt so much better, she'd donned the rest of the outfit—a leather thong and a bra with cut-out nipples. Under her conservative suit, the wild underwear made her feel confident and in control. That would have to do until the new Autumn felt more sure in her skin.

Autumn pasted on her game face—friendly, self-assured and relaxed—and inched her real self back into can't-touch-me safety. *Winners never quit... Fake it till you make it... Go, Autumn, go.*

The fat cat from Evelyn's desk prowled over to her and began to eye her stockings as though they were flesh-filled scratching posts.

Don't even think about it, she silently warned, blocking her legs with her portfolio.

The cat looked at her with regal disdain—*We are not amused*—then launched its bulk onto her lap.

"Oh, excellent," Evelyn exclaimed. "Quincy is particular."

The cat gave her a look: *Very* particular.

Autumn set her portfolio on the adjacent chair and tapped the cat tentatively on the head. "I'm flattered," she said for Evelyn's benefit.

She was kissing up to a *cat?* A hot and heavy cat who was making her thighs sweat and streaking her expensive skirt with orange hair. It would be rude to push him off, so she jiggled her legs to make it less fun to sit on her.

Her move worked and Quincy shot her a jaundiced look, hitched to his feet and plopped onto the other chair, flat on her portfolio. Great.

Strangely enough, though, when next their eyes met,

the cat seemed to want to reassure her. *Relax. He'll be putty in your hands.*

She grinned. Oh, she was in trouble now, accepting a pep talk from a fur-covered blimp whose life likely consisted of long naps punctuated by catnip breaks and the occasional torture of a rodent.

All the same, she felt calmer and when she heard the mayor's footsteps heading her way, she jumped to her feet, ready to demonstrate just how smart and quick and prepared she was for this measly job.

Noticing cat hair on her skirt, she was swiping madly at it when the mayor spoke to her.

"Autumn Beshkin?" He smiled.

She stopped mid-swipe and held out her hand.

Before the mayor shook it a clunk drew their attention. Quincy had pushed her portfolio to the floor.

"Whoops," Autumn said, dropping to get it.

The mayor crouched, too, and before she knew it they were having a tug-of-war over the black leather binder.

She won and they both stood. The mayor looked a little stunned. He probably hadn't expected a wrestling match. "Sorry," he said. "Quincy can be a pest." He held out his hand. "Mike Fields."

She shook his hand, careful to be firm, not knuckle-crunching, as her career prep partner had described her practice handshakes. "Autumn Beshkin."

He looked at her. *Really* looked. Not the usual man stare. More like a therapist or a hypnotist or a priest waiting for a confession. What was the deal with that?

"Pleased to meet you," she said. He was handsome, with even features, a strong jaw, solid mouth and kind eyes that were a deep brown in color. His brown hair was short and slightly curled, not particularly stylish—

neither were his khakis and golf shirt—but he carried himself as though he was used to getting his way without even trying.

"You're not what I expected," he said, almost as if the words surprised him, too.

He didn't expect a stripper, Autumn knew for sure. She'd made Heidi keep her secret. When men found out what she did, they got all dazed and weird and started thinking with their little heads. And that was the last thing she wanted on the first job she would earn with her brains, not her body.

"A P-and-L is a profit and loss statement, not a grocery store," she said levelly. "For a student, I'm experienced. And I am mature, just as Heidi told you."

His eyebrows lifted. "You heard me…?"

"Thin walls." She shrugged.

"Sorry about that. It's just that my sister tends to exaggerate and—"

"Not this time. Not about me. You'll see that, I promise." She stuck her portfolio out at him and held his gaze, determined to convey more confidence than she felt. *He'll be putty in your hands.* But not so far.

"Why don't we step into my office," he said, accepting her shoved portfolio. He looked funny—stunned or annoyed, she couldn't tell.

The needle clicks had stopped dead, so Autumn knew she'd sounded forceful enough to make Evelyn stare. But if you didn't fight for what you wanted, you'd never get it, right?

Autumn threw back her shoulders and strutted past him, ready to kick ass and take names, exactly the way she marched on stage. She was too good for this job, but she was damn well going to get it.

On the other hand, she felt a jolt of regret when the mayor shut the door on Quincy. She needed all the moral support she could get.

MIKE STOOD IN the doorway a second after Autumn passed, fighting for his composure. Had he really said that? *You're not what I expected?* Luckily, she seemed to think he meant her inexperience, not the fact that she was drop-dead gorgeous—a detail Heidi had failed to mention when she'd oversold him on the woman's qualifications.

Appearance was irrelevant to the job, of course, but he'd have liked a heads-up on her beauty. Even worse, while fighting her for her portfolio, he'd caught a glimpse of the sexiest bra he'd ever seen in his life. Black leather and, God help him, open at the tips?

She'd been too busy defending her credentials to notice that he was staring at her as if she was dinner and he was starving. Hell, he was likely to skid on his own drool.

Autumn knows what she's doing, Heidi had told him over the phone. *Oh, yes, she did,* he saw, watching her march into his office, every tilt, sway and twist absolutely intentional. Oh, she knew exactly what she was doing with that body of hers.

But he needed a skilled bookkeeper, not a student hot enough to melt plastic. What he had to do now was send her away without hurting her feelings.

Not easy, he'd bet, since her bravura struck him as something of a bluff. She'd jabbed her portfolio at him like a weapon she wasn't sure would fire.

She sat in his guest chair, crossed a leg with a swishing sound so sexy it hurt his ears and leaned forward.

She was all woman, with great curves, long legs, rust-red hair, a face that belonged in a fashion magazine and big green eyes that took his measure all the way to his socks.

You need it, boy, and soon. And I can give it to you like no one else.

She made him feel as if he'd been alone too long, even though he'd been dating steadily, thanks to the matchmaking service he'd subscribed to six months ago.

There was an edge to her. A mystery. As though she had a very cool secret. Take that bra, for instance. And did her panties match?

Stop thinking with your parts.

Grateful for the desk between them, Mike rested his clasped hands on her leather case. "Heidi told me this internship is important to you."

She leaned forward. "She told me you were desperate."

"In a way, I am. Because Lydia left so suddenly, she didn't have everything in order. The custom software she uses is complex, so I need someone with experience."

"I can handle it. If you'll look at what I brought—" She leaned across his desk to unzip her binder and he closed his eyes against another shot of black leather and pale flesh. He caught her scent, a heady mix of spring rain and spices.

A tapping sound made him open his eyes. She was drumming her index finger on the plastic sheet over her résumé. The fingernail bore a tiny rhinestone in a star pattern. It was blunt-edged. How would those nails feel raking his back?

You're doing it again.

"You can see, I've done bookkeeping for DD Enterprises and here are the classes I've taken so far." She flipped the page. "I've also included a class project." Three pages of a report crackled by. "References from two professors and my employer." Flip. Flip. "And finally, my transcripts. A four-point-oh, as you can see."

"Very impressive—"

"Thank you."

"—for a student," he finished, closing the binder.

Autumn Beshkin fixed him with her fierce green eyes. "I'm fast, I'm resourceful and I'll do what needs to be done."

"I'm sure you would, but I have neither the time nor the knowledge to train you. It's budget time, we're in the middle of an economic development plan, and I'm in charge of the founders celebration—it's our 150th anniversary—a very big deal around here."

"Which means you need someone now. And I'm here. Now."

But he had a call in to a woman who'd recently retired from the Cities and Towns Commission who would do fine. "Look, Ms. Beshkin—"

"Autumn."

"Autumn." Her hair was the color of her name—the striking rust-red of leaves in September. *Stop.* "This job can't be what you want, either. You need a mentor, formal feedback, written evaluations, someone who can spend time with you."

"You're turning me down?" She sounded more outraged than hurt. Like he'd better explain himself and it better be good.

Before he could work up something impressive, Evelyn yelped from the outer office. "Heavenly damn, Quincy!"

Mike rushed out, Autumn at his heels, and found his secretary using her knitting to mop at the laptop she used as her CPU.

"That damn cat knocked over my iced tea!"

Autumn grabbed the laptop and tilted it so the tea trickled from its keyboard. The external keyboard Evelyn used looked untouched. Her monitor, too was all right.

"Is the data backed up?" Mike asked. Evelyn had her own mysterious system of office procedures.

"More or less." Evelyn balled up her knitting.

"Do you have a forced air duster we can dry it with?" Autumn asked. Seeing Evelyn's blank stare, she said, "How about a blow dryer?"

"In the bathroom!" Evelyn ran in that direction.

"Please hold this." Autumn thrust the laptop at him, still tilted, then ran back into his office. She came out with her purse, fished out her keys and detached a small device, which she held up. "This key drive has a gig of memory." She stuck it into a port at the back of the laptop. "Hopefully I can copy the recent files before the motherboard freezes."

Mike set the laptop on a dry spot on Evelyn's desk and Autumn quickly clicked into the hard drive, organizing the files by date. He was impressed by her calm efficiency.

"This way she'll have access until you can service the laptop," she said, still working. "If it's fried, a tech can likely retrieve the files, but who knows when you can get that handled. You have to go to Tucson for service, I imagine."

"True. Good idea. And quick thinking."

"This happened to me at the bar once," she said. "Laptops are convenient, but that also makes them vulnerable."

"I tried to talk Evelyn into a tower, but she likes to stay fast on her feet, she says."

"And I bet keeping Evelyn happy makes everything go smoother around here."

"Exactly." Already, she'd caught the rhythm of the place. They locked gazes and he felt a zip of recognition and pleasure not entirely related to how attractive she was.

He watched Autumn copy the most recent files onto her drive, almost not thinking about her underwear.

She touched her finger to a drop of liquid on the computer, then tasted it. "No sugar. That's good. Stickiness is fatal."

"Yeah," he said, thinking about her tongue. "Fatal."

Evelyn arrived with the dryer and handed it to him. "I need to rinse off my knitting." She bustled away. Evelyn was great with people, but she never let her work interfere with her day. She came through when the chips were down, though. Worked at home on the laptop and read his mind when it counted.

Autumn bent to plug the dryer cord into the power bar and her skirt pulled brutally tight. He looked away, but not before he saw them: black stockings. With seams. And through the slit in her skirt he recognized garters.

Lord God in heaven. Seamed black stockings, garters and a leather cut-out bra. Under that suit, Autumn Beshkin was dressed to kill. Or at least seriously maim. Minimum, make it tough for a man to walk.

She jerked up, surprising him while he was still gawking at her like a kid with his first *Playboy*.

"You okay?" she asked.

"Uh, yeah." He cleared his throat.

"You sure?" A knowing smile teased her lips. Had she noticed the drool?

"I'm, uh, sure."

"If you say so." She waved the dryer at the damp computer, watching him. "You'll want to have the unit serviced, of course. Dried and cleaned thoroughly." She spoke slowly, thoughtfully, playing with something in her mind, he could tell.

He thought about her thoroughly servicing something on him...with her tongue. *Get a grip.*

"Absolutely," he said. "Thanks for, uh, jumping in."

"Whatever you need me to do, Mayor," she said, low and slow, "I will do."

Now Mike Fields was not a guy who made snap decisions or reversed course on a dime. But Autumn Beshkin, standing there in her leather underwear, with her magic key drive and suggestive smile changed all that. "Okay," he said with a sigh, "when can you start?"

2

IT WAS EARLY EVENING when Autumn entered the Copper Corners High auditorium to check on Jasmine, who was at the first rehearsal of the pageant. The job Jasmine had designing costumes would pay for her daughter Sabrina's nearby summer camp since the burlesque revue Autumn and Jasmine were in together was on hiatus for the summer.

Jasmine was fired up about the two friends spending quality time together, but her real purpose for being here was to spend time with her new guy—Mark Fields, brother to Heidi and Mayor Mike.

From close to the stage, Jasmine spotted Autumn and hurried down the aisle carrying a bolt of fabric. "So? Did you get the job?" Jasmine asked, when she was close.

When Autumn nodded, Jasmine whooped, threw down the fabric and hugged Autumn so fast and hard that Autumn accidentally bit her own tongue. "That's so fabulous!" Jasmine said, then leaned back. "Hey, aren't you happy about it?"

"Yeth. Bery ha-y," Autumn said over her aching tongue. Except she was queasy about how she'd gotten the job. She'd caught Mayor Mike in a lust daze and worked it.

Use what you got had always been her philosophy, but using the sex angle had felt like selling out her new self—the woman who got ahead with her brains, not her body.

The idea made her head hurt. Or maybe it was the French braid that she'd pulled so tight her scalp ached. She'd changed into more casual clothes, but had forgotten to let down her hair.

Or maybe it was her reaction to Mayor Mike's lust. She'd felt an answering response that had turned her insides to liquid.

Ridiculous. The man was her *boss*. Completely off-limits, even if she had time for sex. Which she hadn't since she started school.

"So what have you been up to?" Jasmine asked.

Besides seducing the mayor into hiring me? "Not much. I unpacked, did some housework, fed the pets." They'd scored free rent in exchange for doing light housekeeping, watering the plants and taking care of the owners' two cats, freshwater fish tank and a terrarium of turtles and lizards.

"I gave the chuckwalla some meal worms."

"Gross." Jasmine scrunched up her nose.

"Everybody has to eat. Though I don't get the Huffmans. Why spend so much on creatures that couldn't care less?" The Huffmans had bought piles of toys and elaborate hideout towers for their two cats. The fish tank was jammed with plastic plants, a castle and tunnels, and the lizards and turtles had a tiny creek, decorative boulders and miniature hollow logs in their terrarium. The care instructions filled two typed pages.

"I'm sure the animals love them back," Jasmine said.

"With brains the size of kiwi seeds? How much love can there be?"

Jasmine shrugged. "The cats are affectionate."

"When there's food involved, sure." Though Autumn respected a cat's self-sufficiency. If you took care of your own needs, you never got disappointed. "How about you? You're here for the read-through, right? And did you get Sabrina to camp okay?"

"Yes. She made a friend right away. The girl brought the same Bratz doll to camp."

"That's a relief." Autumn worried about Sabrina, who was eleven, pretty and bright, but fought a weight problem, social awkwardness and puberty, which had her giddy with joy one minute, steamrolled by depression the next.

Jasmine tended to gloss over Sabrina's troubles, but Autumn connected with Sabrina—they shared a sense of isolation—and she listened in, advised where she could and felt good that Sabrina saved up her tales of triumph and agony for "Auntie Autumn." Autumn loved that. It made her feel like family. Jasmine said Autumn was Sabrina's *aunt of the heart*, as opposed to her real aunts who were too flaky and selfish to be much support to their niece. Or their sister, for that matter.

"Camp will be good for her," Autumn said. "Fresh air, physical activity, new friends." Summer camp had been one of Jasmine's more sensible ideas. She had a tendency to overspend on Sabrina, though the budget Autumn had helped her with had encouraged her to be more thrifty. Jasmine thanked Autumn over and over for the college savings account that was slowly building.

Jasmine leaned on Autumn for financial advice, support at work and help with Sabrina, but she held her hands to her ears whenever it came to romantic issues.

This latest was the worst. Mark Fields got a walking-into-walls crush on Jasmine after seeing her perform a few months ago. Two short visits and some phone calls later and Jasmine had declared him Mr. Forever.

This worried the hell out of Autumn. Jasmine fell in love too fast and the breakups devastated her. She'd spend days in bed sobbing, blackout curtains in place, leaving poor Sabrina to fend for herself. Autumn always felt so helpless when her friend suffered. And she wanted to kick the shit out of the scumbags who caused it. Each time, Jasmine made Autumn swear: *Never let me do that again. I mean it this time.*

Easier said than done. Jasmine was too much of a romantic. Why couldn't she just accept lust for what it was and not dress it up in a ball gown of love and parade it around?

During the month in Copper Corners, Autumn hoped to help Jasmine ease back into reality—the way you gently guided a sleepwalker back to bed—before things went bad. She worried about Sabrina, who did not need another father figure to disappear as soon as the affair cooled. Which it likely would.

"You have time for dinner?" Autumn asked her.

"Dinner? Uh, well I—" Jasmine blushed "—I'm kind of waiting for Mark. He plays the town founder, Josiah Bremmer. It's the lead. So he's got to be here for the reading."

"Oh. Sure."

"You don't mind," Jasmine said. "Really?"

"I'll grab something at the diner. I want to make it an early night anyway. Maybe I'll study." Now that she'd forced Mike to give her the job, the jitters had started up. Working for Copper Corners would not be as simple as tracking the receipts at the strip club for Duke. She would be accountable for the entire town's finances. There were budgets to wrangle and Lydia's complex software to figure out.

She didn't dare screw up. She needed the mayor's recommendation for her class and her résumé. Plus, she'd practically strong-armed him into hiring her. Her pride was at stake.

"How's this going?" she asked Jasmine, nodding toward the lit stage, where people stood talking, scripts in hand. Two young guys banged away on a rickety-looking covered wagon, while two girls painted saguaro cactus onto a backdrop of a pink-and-orange desert sunset.

"They're waiting for Mark to start." Jasmine sighed like an obsessed fan.

"It looks fun." Autumn loved the feel of the theater—the bright-white lights, the black-painted stage, the smells of wood and linen and paint and pancake makeup. She'd discovered the glory of it when she got a part in a high school musical, but that was an old story that had ended all wrong.

She felt similarly when she performed in the three-woman burlesque revue with Jasmine, who did their costumes, and Nevada Neru, their choreographer. The revue had opened last year to rave reviews and had drawn steady crowds all season. She loved the excitement, the magic, the rapt faces of the audience. When she performed she felt so alive.

She enjoyed the revue better than straight stripping, she'd concluded, because they were a team and their dances were more complex and told a story.

"There's the director, Sheila," Jasmine said, pointing to a blond woman who was gesturing dramatically as she talked to the actors on stage. "She wants to meet you."

"You didn't tell her, did you?"

"That you're a stripper? No. I promised I wouldn't."

"Good. And no telling Mark, either." Autumn had been off the night Mark saw the revue, so, if Jasmine kept her promise, Autumn could remain incognito while she was here.

"You're safe," Jasmine said in a stage whisper. "No one knows that inside the chest of an ordinary accountant beats the heart of a man-killing pole dancer."

"And let's keep it that way," Autumn said.

"I don't know why it's such a big deal. Sheila thinks it's great that I'm a stripper. She auditioned to be a Vegas showgirl, you know."

"You give people too much credit, Jasmine. Strippers scare the hell out of women and turn men into slathering beasts."

"What the hell is slather? Is it sweat or drool?"

"You're ignoring my point."

"Whatever. How does the mayor seem as a boss?" Jasmine asked, doing it again.

"It's too soon to tell." Heidi had described Mike as *everybody's big brother,* and in just the few minutes it took Autumn to fill out payroll papers, she'd seen that. Mike had taken several calls that all ended in him offering some kind of help, then headed out to discuss a property dispute between two ranchers.

"I wonder what's keeping Mark?" Jasmine looked up the burgundy-carpeted aisle toward the auditorium door, practically quivering in anticipation.

As if on cue, the door opened and two men entered—Mike and a guy who looked like a smaller version of him carrying an armload of books.

"There he is," Jasmine breathed.

Autumn enjoyed what she could see of the night sky through the doorway before it shut. One nice thing about a tiny town—its few lights didn't interfere with the darkness so the sky could show off all its stars, millions of tiny pin-pricks in the velvet vastness. The big sky almost made up for the small minds.

The brothers loped toward them. Autumn was annoyed to realize that watching Mike approach had her holding her breath.

"Well, hello," Mike said. He seemed surprised to see her there. "This is Autumn Beshkin, Mark. She's taking over for—" He turned to his brother, who was busy staring at Jasmine.

"Missed you," Mark whispered.

"Me, too," Jasmine said, looking at him as though she wanted to swallow him whole. They'd seen each other the night before. How could they miss each other?

"Give her the books," Mike muttered, elbowing his brother in a way that showed he was annoyed, too.

"Books? Yeah, sure." Mark extended his armload. "Here's the town history, some Web sites and stuff on old mining towns."

"Thank you, Mark. So much." You'd think he'd given her an orgasm.

"That's a lot of reading," Autumn observed.

"I want my costumes to be authentic."

"Don't you have to get up there?" Mike said to his brother, nodding toward the stage.

"Yeah," Mark said, his eyes glued to Jasmine.

"The director's heading over here," Autumn said, rolling her eyes. She caught Mike doing the same. She hoped it was because of how silly these two were behaving and not because he disapproved of Jasmine.

"There you are, Mark!" Sheila chirped. "We need you on stage. If we can pry you away from our costume designer here." She smiled indulgently at them both. Already Sheila knew about the affair. So much for discretion.

Sheila turned to Mike. "What brings you here, Mayor? Are you interested in a part, too? I think we could fit you in if—"

"No, no. Please. Just want to be sure you have what you need, Sheila, for the production."

"So far, so good. I'm thrilled to have a real costumer. I'm still pinching myself. Plus the president of the Chamber of Commerce as our star? I'm simply stunned by my good fortune. Simply *stunned*."

"We all are stunned." Mike shot his brother a look. "Considering how busy the guy is with his real estate business and his town committees."

"Oh, he's very, very busy, all right." Sheila winked and she clearly meant an entirely different kind of *busy*.

Mike frowned. "So the budget is fine?" he asked Sheila, obviously to change the subject.

"You have enough money for the fabrics, Jasmine?" Sheila asked.

There was a pause while Jasmine seemed to descend from her pink cloud. "Hmm? Oh, uh, yes. I'll have sketches soon. This is my friend, Autumn Beshkin, Sheila."

"So pleased to meet you," Sheila said, shaking Autumn's hand with both of hers. "We're so grateful to have your talented friend with us. Aren't we lucky she had time to do our pageant?" She turned to the brothers.

"Very lucky," Mark said, looking moonstruck.

Good freakin' Lord. Autumn caught Mike's look. He seemed to feel the same as she did.

"So, shall we get started? Hmm?" Sheila sang, holding out her arms to shoo Jasmine and Mark before her like baby chicks.

"Let me know if you need anything else, Sheila," Mike said.

"Count on it," Sheila said, the airy music gone from her voice. Beneath the sugary gratitude was a woman who would kick ass when necessary. That made Autumn smile.

Mike turned to her. "Like I said, this festival's big— one-five-oh. Sesquicentennial, though everyone says 'Huh?' when you use that word. Big budget, fancy pageant and a full festival."

"And you're in charge?"

"That's what they tell me." He spoke as though it was a burden, but she could tell he wouldn't have it any other way.

She understood. Nevada and Jasmine sometimes accused her of running the revue when she filled in the gaps. Her official job was promotion and scheduling, but she did what needed to be done. "I'm here to help however you need me."

"Yeah." In the cool dimness of the auditorium, he

gave her that look again. Saw right into her. She'd never felt that before with a man and it startled her. For a second, she seemed to be floating in a pale version of Jasmine's pink cloud. Weird.

Mike seemed to jolt back to normal himself. "So, have you eaten?"

"Not yet, no."

"How about I treat you to dinner? We can go to Louie's if you like Italian. Yolanda's Cocina, the diner down the street, has Mexican food. Got a write-up in *Tucson Weekly,* mostly for the kitschy artwork."

"The diner sounds good," she said, ignoring the steady buzz of attraction in her head. This was not a good idea.

She needed to eat, didn't she? And the better she knew the mayor, the easier it would be to give him what he wanted at work, right? She could ferret out job details. Sure.

And enjoy his wry smile, intense eyes and nice smell....

Lord, she was acting just like Jasmine.

3

THE MINUTE THEY stepped into the funky diner, Autumn felt at home. She loved the campy velvet paintings on the wall and the shelves overflowing with Mexican handicrafts—brightly painted skulls, *Día de los Muertos* tableau and statues of *La Virgen*. She even liked the mariachi music blasting loud enough to rattle her fillings.

A gray-haired woman wearing an apron headed their way, then stopped to yell over her shoulder. "Goddammit, Rosalva, we're going deaf."

Smiling at them, she spoke in a normal tone. "Sit toward the back, Mike, would you? Esther's still swole up from that abscess, so I'm running my stumps off."

"Sure thing, Suze." Mike led Autumn down the aisle, greeting everyone he passed, asking questions and answering the ones he was asked. He introduced Autumn as Lydia's fill-in. Autumn felt curious looks follow them to the back booth.

"Tongues are wagging now," Mike said, shaking his head.

"Why is that?"

"Because you're gorgeous and I'm not married."

"These people need to get lives."

But he looked suddenly serious. "Listen, Autumn,

if I made you uncomfortable today in any way, I apologize." Color shot up his neck and he looked utterly shame-faced.

"You didn't," she said, not ready to point out the fact that she'd taken advantage of his weakness.

"I'm not usually like that."

"It's okay. Really." The man was apologizing for the one thing she completely understood—he was a male animal with a sex drive. There was nothing wrong with that at all.

In fact, her body was celebrating his masculinity this very instant. Her skin felt hot, her nerves jumpy and she crossed her legs against the swelling ache in her sex.

Not helpful at all. She was supposed to pick her boss's brains, not jump his bones.

"I'm glad to hear that." Mike handed her a laminated menu. "Look this over, but you'll want the chiles rellenos, medium spice and a nopalitos-and-goat-cheese salad."

"What makes you so sure?"

"I just know." He winked as though he'd figured her out right down to her taste in Mexican food. Attraction zipped between them, making the candle flicker. Or maybe that was how unnaturally hard she was breathing.

Settle down.

"How about because it's the next best thing to our machaca burros, which we're usually out of this time of night?" Suze said in a raspy voice, talking around a cigarette, which wagged as she talked.

"There's that." Mike grinned.

"We only offer the one salad," she added. "It's a good one but it's all she wrote."

"Guess that's what I'll have then," Autumn said.

"Double it," Mike said. "And two Tecates." He looked at Autumn. "Goes great."

"Is he right, Suze?" Autumn asked, getting into the down-home attitude.

Suze winked. "Comin' right up." She left and their gazes collided, then bounced away. Hers landed on the art on the wall behind him. It was a velvet painting of Elvis as a bullfighter, smart and ironic. She smiled. "I like the art in here."

Mike turned to see what she was looking at. "We may only have two streetlights, but we know our velvet paintings."

"Evidently. They're all around." She looked around the place. "You've possibly cornered the market."

"We should put that on our Web site. Could bring us some art lovers."

"You're always thinking about your job, huh?"

"I'm the official town worrier."

"Is there a lot to worry about?"

"Enough. We need business growth badly. Our bank is losing customers to the big chains. The grocery and hardware stores struggle. People tend to shop in Tucson. The idea is to give people reasons to spend their money in town, churn it back into our pockets."

As he talked, he fiddled with his silverware and she couldn't take her eyes off his round-tipped fingers. He shifted his weight on the bench, moving with an athlete's restlessness. He was well-built, so what did he do for exercise?

Stop staring at the man.

"That's easy enough to understand," she said, focusing in.

"But people don't think like that. They think about saving money or buying what they want, or getting a good selection."

She nodded, conceding his point about human nature.

Suze arrived with their beers and Mike asked the woman about her son, who'd recently left town. She seemed to miss him and Mike's expression was full of compassion. When Suze left, Mike looked out around the place, checking on everyone, as if to see that all was well.

Which turned out to be kind of sexy.

Like everything else about the man.

"So, enough about my headaches," he said. "Tell me about yourself. You're in school to become a CPA?" He caught her gaze. Again he really looked at her. Like a shrink or a father confessor or a man who knew her more intimately than any man ever had.

He made her feel soft and he made her feel wanted. She longed to reach out to touch his tan cheek, brush the fan of crinkles at the corners of his eyes.

"That's the plan," she said instead, drinking some beer to distract herself.

"Have you always loved numbers?" He leaned forward, his expression earnest, as though he really wanted to know.

"I guess." It had taken an embarrassingly long time for her to see how her gift with figures could become a profession.

"And…?"

"Nothing. I just…I guess I love the orderliness of numbers, knowing that the formulas always work and if you don't make mistakes, it all comes out right."

"Makes sense." He tilted his head at her, as if figuring her out. "So, after you get your degree, what's the plan then?"

"Then I get a job with a big firm, get some solid experience, network like crazy until I make enough contacts and save enough to open my own business."

"You'd rather work for yourself?"

"Oh, yeah. I want my own clients, you know? People who depend on me. I want to help them maximize their income, minimize their taxes, get them where they want to be financially, all that. I want them to count on me, you know?"

She was surprised how easy it was to blurt the ideas she'd always kept in her head, thinking them over and over when school got hard or she got worried and lost sleep.

"So it's not just the numbers," he said slowly. "It's also helping people."

"Yeah. I guess that's it. When I helped Jasmine figure out a budget and it worked for her, I really liked that. Now she's saving money for college for her daughter. So, yeah, I suppose it's that the numbers mean something to people, you know?"

"I do."

She was suddenly embarrassed by how she sounded—eager as a kid, which was kind of how she felt in her classes. Very different from her usual guarded self. She hardly knew Mike and yet she was telling him all this. "Anyway, the point is I want a private practice."

"I bet you'll do great." He said it so simply, so sincerely that warmth flooded her.

He has no idea who you are, she reminded herself.

She was about to blurt the doubts bubbling under her words when Suze saved her by bringing the food.

Which turned out to be great. The chiles rellenos melted in her mouth, the nopalitos-and-goat-cheese salad was tangy and fresh.

"So, what all is Lydia responsible for?" she asked, hoping to find out enough to reassure herself for tomorrow.

"Too much." Mike sighed. "Budgets, purchasing, fees and licenses, billings. You'll see tomorrow. I don't know half of the stuff she does." He shook his head and took a bite, oblivious to the fact that his words had stopped her heart.

What if she wasn't up to it? What if she was all just big talk? What if she let Mike and the town down?

"Hey, Mayor. How's it hanging?"

Mike looked up from a bite of salad to greet the man who'd stopped at their table. "Hey, Ned," he said. "How's the welcome sign coming along?"

"We'll have it done for the festival. No worries."

"Good." Mike introduced her to Ned Langton, who'd bought Mike's family's landscaping business a few years back.

"So, I tried to join your Chamber last night," Ned drawled, an amused grin on his face, "but couldn't get your brother to give me the time of day."

"Oh, yeah?" Mike stopped chewing.

"Couldn't take his hands off his girl long enough to round up the form for me."

"I see." Mike set down his fork, his mouth grim, despite his easy words. "Stop by tomorrow and Evelyn can fix you up."

"What I want to know is where he found her." Ned

leaned lower and winked, "And are there any more where she came from?"

"With a wife like Jill, why would you think twice, Ned?" There was an edge to Mike's words.

"I'm not thinking about me. She got a friend for *you?* That's what I mean."

·Mike shot an apologetic glance at Autumn. "I don't know, Ned, but how about you write me a check for Chamber dues and we'll mail you the temporary card. Save you time. How's that?"

Ned didn't like that suggestion, it seemed. He patted his shirt pocket and frowned sheepishly. "Left my checkbook at the house. I'll stop by another day. Enjoy your dinner."

"You called his bluff," Autumn said when Ned had gone.

"Yeah." He gave a rueful smile. "It's pulling teeth to get these guys to join up. The Chamber funds economic projects and we really need everyone to ante up, but they don't all see it."

"That's not what's bothering you though, is it?"

"No. It's my brother." He shook his head. "Seems like the affair's all over town. Since he met your friend, his brains have drained out his ears."

"How so?" She hoped he wasn't about to insult Jasmine.

"The minute Mark heard Jasmine was doing the pageant, he auditioned for it. What was he thinking? He's got a business to run, he's head of the Chamber and chair of my economic development committee. He doesn't have time to be in a *play,* for God's sake." He shook his head.

"Maybe it's true love."

He shot her a look. "Your friend is a beautiful woman."

"You mean she's a stripper." Anger flared, fast and hot as a suddenly lit match.

He quirked a brow. "I don't care what she does for a living. The problem is how fast this is going."

She just looked at him.

"Come on. You were rolling your eyes right along with me. They're acting like a couple of teenagers. The man came back from a weekend in Phoenix and declared his dreams had come true. Lord."

"Yeah," she said, softening. "I know what you mean. Jasmine falls in love with love and gets hurt every time."

"The thing is…" He hesitated. "Mark was like this once before." He frowned and picked at his Tecate label. "He met this woman at a real estate seminar and right off he's loaning her money and they're talking about buying a house. Then he finds out she's got a husband in Nevada and a check fraud conviction. Took him years to get over her."

"That's too bad."

"Yep. And he's wild like that about your friend."

"Look, Jasmine is a good person. She—"

"I'm sure she is. It's just too fast and crazy. It's—"

"Reckless. I know. They barely know each other. They're telling themselves fairy tales."

"Exactly," he said. "So we're both worried about them."

"Yeah," she said, relieved that Mike's concerns matched her own. "I mean if it's right, why not slow down?"

"There you go. Just what I told him."

They shared a smile of commiseration.

"Hey, Mayor Mike!" A stylish blonde stopped at their booth, her arm around the waist of a tall guy in a cowboy hat.

"Celia. Hi," Mike said. "Dan." He nodded at the man.

"So, that sister of yours pregnant yet?" Celia asked him.

"You'll know before me," he said. "We both know that."

Autumn recognized Celia's name. She owned the beauty salon where Heidi had worked before moving to Phoenix.

"I want you to meet Autumn Beshkin," Mike said. "She's filling in for Lydia."

"Autumn… I know that name…."

"Heidi's a friend of mine. She does my hair." She spoke fast, praying Heidi hadn't mentioned what Autumn did for a living. She pushed a strand of hair into her braid.

"We miss Heidi so much," Celia said. "Her counseling almost more than her hair work. She left us her self-help books when she went to Phoenix, but it's not the same."

Heidi was studying to become a therapist, Autumn knew. In fact, Heidi had helped convince Autumn she belonged in college.

"When you get us a regular clinic, Mike, get us a shrink, too, wouldja?" Celia said.

"I'll do my best," he said. "We need a bigger population to keep a full-time doc busy."

"I'm just teasing. Criminy Christmas, Mike, lighten up. He's so serious all the time." Celia smiled at Autumn. "I mean, heck, if you can't laugh at yourself then everyone else will just have to do it behind your back."

"I'm sure they already do, Celia." Mike sighed.

"Cheer him up, would you?" she said to Autumn. "How long will you be here?"

"Just until Lydia gets back," Mike said. "A month."

"Don't be rushing a new mother back on the job, Mayor Mike. Not everyone lives for council meetings. Maybe Autumn can stick around longer." She smiled at her.

"This is just an internship. School starts up again soon. And I have a job." They'd booked rehearsals for the new season of the revue right after the pageant was over.

"Well, shoot. Too bad you can't stay. At the very least, maybe you can talk the man into getting a bowling team together. He's got a good arm."

"Hmm." She looked at Mike.

"I'm too busy," he said, lifting his hands as if for mercy.

"We've got a tournament coming. This boy needs a life. See if you can convince him."

"I'll try." Autumn smiled and Celia and Dan moved on. "So, is she right?" she asked him, resting her chin on her fist.

"About my bowling? I do okay."

"No, that you need a life."

He shrugged. "Celia likes to pick at you till you bleed," he said. "I hope you don't need your hair done while you're here. The Cut 'N Curl is a hive."

"I think I'm fine." She touched her hair.

"Yeah. Your hair is—nice. I, uh, like the color." His tan darkened with blush.

The sexual vibe, a low rumbling between them as they'd talked, revved fiercely.

"Thanks. It's natural." Why had she said that? In her world, most strippers had extensions, blond dye jobs and fake boobs, so she took pride in what nature gave her. But Mike didn't know that, nor would he care.

"So you won't need the salon." His voice was low, full of leashed heat. She pictured him freeing her hair, running his fingers through the strands, his eyes hungry. "That's lucky." He seemed to force out a laugh. "The place is like a cross between Jerry Springer and Dr. Phil. I don't know why that happens."

"It's because this is a small town." She knew that from her mother's stories. "Doesn't it bug you that everyone knows your business?" The idea seemed suffocating to her.

"It can, I guess. It depends. Are you from a small town?"

"No. My mom was and she hated it." Anne Muldoon grew up in a trailer on the grimy side of town with a reputation as a tramp with a temper. The chip on her shoulder never went away, even after she moved to Phoenix, where she eventually married Autumn's father, Adam Beshkin. She chased him away when Autumn was twelve, almost triumphant when he left.

You can only count on yourself in this world, Autumn. Don't kid yourself different. Decent advice, Autumn knew, despite her mother's bitterness.

"Small towns aren't for everyone," Mike said.

"That's not very visitor's bureau-like of you, Mayor Mike. Shouldn't you promote the low crime rate, the neighborliness—an entire town where everybody knows your name?" She used a teasing tone. She didn't hate small towns the way her mother did, but she saw their limits and certainly didn't want to end up in one.

He shrugged. "It's a closed system. There's not much privacy. People have history and long memories."

"Yeah. My mom felt kind of second class and I guess that's how they treated her."

"So you grew up where? Phoenix?"

"Yes." She'd experienced the pain and trap of reputation in high school, which was its own brand of small town. In truth, Autumn never felt as though she fit anywhere. "But you like it here, right? You're the mayor."

"Yeah. And I'm lucky I can afford to do it full time. My goal is to boost our economy, but it's a tough go."

"How so?"

"Attracting new business isn't easy for small towns. We almost scored a herbal tea factory, but the company balked over helping to extend the water lines. Then, because we lost the factory, the motel chain that was looking at us evaporated. The domino effect."

"That would be discouraging."

"If we could get some grants, that would help. But I need time to work up the proposals. Meanwhile, our police department needs a new computer system and we've got to replace the fire trucks and—" Mike shot her a look. "I've been going on and on," he said softly. "Sorry."

"No, no. I'm very interested. Part of my internship is to become aware of the context of my work. We aren't just about the numbers, you know."

He smiled. "So there's more to you than meets the eye." There was a teasing, sexual tone to his words. They'd fallen easily into that mode of relating.

"I would hope so," she said in the same tone. "How about you? Are you a complicated man?"

"Not at all." He grinned.

But she knew that wasn't quite true and she was curious. Too curious. Maybe because of how easy it was to talk to him, to think out loud with him, the way he listened so closely.

As the meal had continued, the gaps in their conversation had been filled with knowing glances and a building tension that was difficult to ignore.

Mike paid the tab for dinner and they stepped out into the warm summer night. Streetlights lit the sidewalk and the full moon glowed silver overhead, surrounded by distant stars in a black, black sky.

Under the cooking smells from the restaurant, Autumn picked up the welcome scent of desert dust and creosote. To her it was the smell of home.

She was full of good food and just a little buzzed from the Tecates, so that when Mike turned to her, ready to end the evening, she said, "So what do folks do for fun around here?"

"You mean besides watch the grass grow and peer at the neighbors through binoculars?" His tone held self-mockery with an edge of cynicism. He wasn't entirely thrilled with small town life either, she guessed.

"Besides that," she said.

"Okay, let's see." He stared off into the sky, silhouetted against the blackness. "For music, there's a mariachi group that plays weekends. A local boy has a jazz trio that plays at Louie's Italian Place on Thursday nights."

"So there's a music scene. What else?"

"The Brew and Cue for pool at the far end of town. There's bowling, like Celia mentioned. Wicked Skeeball tourneys at the Green Dragon Pizzeria. High school sports. Tours of the historic district, including the Copper Strike Mine. Our prickly pear candy factory, Cactus Confections, has some regional fame."

He shrugged. "Not much, huh? You'll find what you want in Tucson, Autumn."

"And what is it you think I want?" She spoke lightly, but sexual energy underlined her words. Maybe she should have stopped at one beer.

"Nightclubs, concerts, plays, movies." He shrugged.

"You go to Tucson for those things?"

"When I have time, sure."

"But not often, I can tell. You're all about work, I bet."

"You got me. I play basketball with my brother once in a while. Watch sports, rent movies. Now and then, though, I go out to the resort outside town—Desert Paradise—and hit golf balls. The grass is dead—the place is closed—so I kick up some dust, but there's nothing like it for getting rid of frustration."

"You have a lot of that? Frustration?" The tease hung in the warm air between them.

"My share." He winked. "Uneasy lies the head that wears a crown—even a little crown." She liked that he didn't take himself seriously. She wished she were that easy on herself.

"To tell you the truth, I'd love to find a buyer for the resort. It would be a shot in the arm for our economy. We've had inquiries, but no real offers. It's a beautiful property. Well laid out. Lots of potential."

"Sounds nice."

Silence fell. She should go home, get some sleep before her first day of work, but something hovered in the air between them, energy and possibility, and she wanted to pursue it, as crazy and wrong as that might be.

"Take me out there," she heard herself say.

"You want to go to the resort?"

"Sure. Show me all that economic potential."

"It's dark." But he was smiling.

"There's a moon. Come on."

He paused, studied her, then nodded. "Okay. Sure."

His startled delight overcame her doubts. This might be a bad idea, but at the moment, it seemed worth the risk.

4

AUTUMN CLIMBED INTO Mike's sleek and sexy Saab
9-2X wagon—weren't these cars designed by jet en-
gineers?—and they drove with the windows down, the
sunroof open, allowing the warm breeze to blow
through and the stars to spin by overhead.

"I've never been here at night," Mike said, turning
at the sign marking the entrance to the Desert Paradise
Golf Resort. He parked in the gravel lot and opened her
door for her. She climbed out and looked around. The
moon was bright enough to let her see the main
building, the casitas, the courts, the empty pool.

A gravel path lined by mile-high date palms led to
the golf course. It was quiet except for the crunch of
their feet in the gravel and the distant swish of cars on
the highway. Soon they reached the clubhouse parking
lot. Before them lay the low rolling hills of the course.
Here and there were stands of eucalyptus and mesquite
trees, along with landscaped areas.

A puff of warm air lifted her hair and she smelled the
iron and earth of the pond, which, because it was part
of the area's irrigation system, still held water, Mike had
explained. It was a smear of shiny darkness ahead of
them. Without rain, the grass was short and dry.

"It's peaceful out here," she said, tilting her head up

at the moon, very conscious of Mike's closeness, the way he tracked her every move. It was almost embarrassing how alive she felt standing here with him.

"Puts things in perspective," he said, looking at her.

And made the attraction more vivid, she realized, dragging her eyes from his face. "I love summer nights in the desert. There's still heat, but it's gentler, like the desert is saying, *You put up with my broiler all day, so take a breather, relax, enjoy the beauty, the silence, the serenity.*"

"Very poetic."

"Not really. I just love the desert, I guess." She paused. "So hitting balls gets rid of frustration, huh? Maybe we should send Jasmine and Mark out here."

"I'm afraid they're too far gone."

"Love at first sight, according to Jasmine."

"Do you believe in that?"

"Not really. Though an attraction can be intense." Like the one between them at the moment.

"Yeah, it can." His voice was so low and heated that her stomach dropped to her knees.

"So, what does one do about that?" She was grateful the moon wasn't bright enough to reveal the hot blush on her cheeks. She wasn't one for turning red, but right now she felt like a stoplight.

"Hope it burns out before anyone gets hurt," he said.

"Is that the voice of experience?"

"You mean have I ever had my heart broken?" He smiled wryly. "I've avoided that mistake. How about yourself?"

"I've managed." She'd had a couple of close calls. The first guy—Anton—seemed to like that she was a stripper and she'd let her guard down. When his parents planned a trip out to see him, she'd redecorated her living room, bought good china, planned a gourmet meal, even though she was a shitty cook.

Meanwhile, he stopped calling. Returned after his parents left with some lame excuse and she knew she was his girl on the side, his secret vice. She'd been hurt, insulted, pissed, told him to go screw himself. Mostly, she was furious at herself for going blind, for being weak.

She'd been a mess in the aftermath, barely recognizable as the kick-ass woman she worked so hard every day to be.

The second guy was a skirt-chaser, who reformed for her until she caught him with a day-shift dancer. He'd begged for forgiveness, complaining about all the temptations at the club. What flipped her out was how much she'd built her life around him, nested in, building a house of matchsticks, ready to explode with a bit of friction on a hard surface.

Since then, she'd kept it simple with guys who wanted only a hot connection, no morning-after calls and no regrets. And since starting school, she'd had no interest in even that and sex had been on the back burner.

She didn't want to talk about any of her history with Mike, so she shifted the focus to him. "I would think you'd have a Mrs. Mayor by now."

"I'd like that. Very much." His abrupt vulnerability surprised her. She'd expected a teasing reply.

"Really?"

"I haven't had a lot of free time."

"There's always time to—date." Or to have sex at least. Though maybe Mayor Mike was old-fashioned. Maybe he dated a respectful number of times before he got naked with a woman.

Mmm, naked. Don't picture him. Don't. Don't.

"I've made it a priority the last few months, but nothing serious so far."

"I can't imagine the single women of Copper Corners aren't lining up for the mayor."

He grimaced. "I don't want women lining up."

"No social climbers need apply?"

"The town has a population of twelve hundred, Autumn. Mostly families. Single people head for the cities. And, as to social climbing, we're pretty much a single-story town."

"There's always a ladder, Mike. Don't kid yourself." She knew that from hanging on the bottom rungs in high school and later, as a stripper, set apart from the straight world, even though she knew herself to be a moral person.

"I don't treat people that way." He held her gaze, telling her he meant it. There was something rock-solid about the guy. She still didn't want to hear his opinion of her other career. He might disappoint her and she wanted to respect him a while longer. At least as long as she worked for him.

"What are you looking for in a wife?" she asked.

"What you'd expect. A partner, someone with similar values and interests, someone committed to family and home."

"What about looks? Attraction? Passion?"

He shrugged. "That's part of it."

"But mainly, you want someone to bake your bread and match your socks and keep the home fires burning?" She was teasing, but she felt an undercurrent of irritation and…envy? What was that about? She would never tolerate life as some man's *little woman*. That would be a prison sentence—life without parole.

Of course men weren't lining up to ask her to bake them pies, by any means. Autumn was all about sex and heat and animal drives. And she liked that, knew that, trusted how it worked. It was simple and human and satisfying.

She loved that she could render men speechless and desperate with a slow spin, a soft slide, a loosened bra. She loved that a hint of nakedness, the suggestion of contact, made them as hard as the chrome poles she danced around. She loved that.

"I'm not sure what you're getting at, but I want an equal partner, not domestic help."

"So you're willing to share your pants?"

"If she's into that, sure," he said, making it sound deliciously sexual. His joke showed her he wasn't a secret chauvinist. "What about you? What do you want in a husband?"

"I don't want a husband. Or a boyfriend for that matter. Sometimes being alone is…better." Maybe she didn't know the difference between lust and love. Or maybe she was like her friend Sugar and didn't have the happily-ever-after gene. Well, the old Sugar, anyway.

Mike looked thoughtful. *Please don't say it,* she silently begged him. *A woman as beautiful as you shouldn't be alone…People need people, blah, blah, blech.*

Instead, he laughed, the sound warm and rich on the quiet desert air. "Good point. If I had a beer, I'd drink to that."

"Hear, hear," she said, pretending to lift a glass.

He tapped his knuckles against hers.

Heat zinged between them. They both looked away.

Standing close to Mike, breathing in synch, swaying closer with each heartbeat, Autumn's back-burner sex drive was suddenly boiling all over the stove, flooding the floor and scalding her toes.

Sex with Mike would be different, unexpected, she could tell. It would be like wading into a lake and having the bottom suddenly drop out from under her.

"You're in school now, anyway," Mike said. "It's not the right time to settle down."

She didn't argue, though she didn't see marriage in her future. A steady lover might be nice if they could keep it simple. Her mother had been right. It was far better to count on yourself. If you started depending on a man, you got soft and lost your edge and your way.

"So, you're enjoying school?" he asked.

"Very much." So much it embarrassed her. She was wildly proud of her grades, lapped up her professors' praise like a cream-hungry cat. "I'm older than most of the students, but I don't care. I can't believe how they take college for granted. They're all living off daddy's money, too busy partying to study. I love every lecture. I even love studying. I'm soaking it all up, you know? Sometimes, I forget to eat. I—" She stopped, embarrassed again. The guy made her too comfortable blurting out secrets. "Sorry. Got carried away."

"I think it's great, Autumn. I'd like to be that fired up about something."

"You love being mayor, don't you?"

"Sure." He hesitated. "Maybe I just take it for granted. Maybe you'll rub off on me."

"Maybe." The idea of rubbing *against* the man made her weak in the knees and she took a shuddering breath.

"So, you met Heidi at her salon, but what work did

you do before you started school? I forget what your résumé said."

She'd only listed her bookkeeping for Moons—the DD in DD Enterprises stood for the owner, Duke Dunmore. "I had bar experience." Which was true.

"Ah, a waitress."

She didn't correct him. She *had* been a cocktail waitress, but when she needed money to keep her little brother out of trouble, she'd hit amateur night at a strip club. It took two shots of tequila and a muscle relaxant to endure the surreal embarrassment of teasing off her clothes in the hot, close quiet of men's staring lust, but she'd done it, by God.

Took first place and the club owner offered her a job.

She'd found her game face, too—adding a sexy element to the mask she wore as a girl to get along with her angry mother. The trick with stripping was to offer the teasing possibility of sex, but always hold back your soul.

The money was great and she made friends among the dancers, DJs and bartenders. It could be a dark life. Some strippers used drugs or hooked on the side, but that wasn't Autumn.

"Good for you for trying for more," Mike said. "Sometimes I think about going back to school. I only did junior college. Mark and I had a deal—two years each—so we could keep the family landscaping business going."

"What would you study if you went back?"

"I don't know. Civic leadership. Or business. Hell, not too ambitious, huh? What's the point? I have obligations."

"The point is to do what makes you happy, not just

what people expect." She'd only begun to learn that lesson.

"I'm needed. That's important to me."

She admired his sense of duty. "But what you want matters, too. What do you wish you could do? Really?"

"Lord." He looked up at the sky, then back down at her. "There have been things I gave up, I guess."

"Like what?"

"I always wanted to get my pilot's license. But it takes time and it's expensive. Hell, for that matter, I'd love to learn to hang glide."

"You want to hang glide?"

"Yeah. I took a ride with a pilot once. It's so quiet and very free. You feel like you've escaped."

"Is that what you want? To escape your life?"

He laughed. "Maybe I just need a vacation."

"Or maybe more." She felt his yearning like heat on her skin. In the moonlight, his eyes looked like diamonds bubbling in melted chocolate and the sight gave her a twisting sensation in her middle—part longing, part desire.

"Anyway, here's where I tee off." He kicked at the rubber mat at their feet, changing the subject.

"So you aim out there?" She squinted out into the darkness. "Too bad we don't have a club and some balls."

"We couldn't see where they landed."

"So what? Just let it fly." Out here under the wide, star-scattered sky, she felt so free. Anything seemed possible. "I bet I could hit a hole in one in the dark."

"You know what? I just bet you could." He stepped closer.

The breeze lifted her hair, snagging a strand on her lip. Mike brushed it away with gentle fingers, taking care of her the way he took care of the town. She felt the heat of his touch for long seconds. His diamond-chocolate eyes glittered at her, wanting her. He tilted his face, leaned closer. He wanted to kiss her.

And she wanted him to.

Why not? It was as if the whole evening had built to this moment. They were in a tiny time warp where this couldn't possibly be wrong.

Normally, she would make the move, but this time she wanted to be kissed, to be swept away by Mike's mouth, by his desire for her. She closed her eyes, parted her lips and waited. How would he kiss her? Soft or urgent? Gentle or fierce? Would he just use his lips or tease with his tongue, too? She hoped—

"Hang on," Mike said.

She opened her eyes to see him galloping toward his car. God, had she scared him away? But then she saw him grab something out of his trunk—two golf clubs and two boxes of balls. He ran back to her, looking so good— his upper body tight and controlled, his gait easy, as though he could go for miles without breaking a sweat.

"Let's do it," he said when he reached her. "Let's hit balls into the dark." He didn't seemed to have noticed she'd pooched her lips out at him. Good. Better, really. Less complicated.

"I've only played miniature golf," she said.

"Close enough. Let me show you." He demonstrated the grip, the stance, the swing. She'd never thought golf was particularly sexy, but the way Mike's body twisted, muscles graceful with power, made her sex ache and her stomach melt. She'd love to see that body naked, wrapped around her, not a golf club.

"Want to try?" he asked, handing her the club.

Oh, yeah. "Sure." She focused on getting the hang of a swing, which he'd made look easy. Her first tries were shaky and tentative, but soon she was ready to try hitting a ball.

"I've got two boxes of three balls, two brands, so we can tell them apart when we come back to see how we did." He put the first ball on a tee. "You go first."

"About where is the hole?"

When he pointed, his arm brushed her cheek. The sensation made her feel faint, but she prepared to swing, the swish of wind through the mesquites making her feel so light, she was afraid she could be blown away, too.

She wished Mike would put his arms around her, under the pretense of helping her, just to feel his skin against hers, but this had to be her own wild swing into the night.

"Here goes." She pulled back her club, kept her eye on the ball and swung with all her might. There was a thwack, the blow vibrated the club in her hand, and the ball arced in a high curve she followed until it disappeared into the inky dark.

Mike whistled. "You're a natural, lady."

"That felt good." She laughed with pleasure. "Now you go."

He set up and swung, the ball flying higher than hers, but disappearing at the same point in the darkness. "You're right. That does feel good."

He set up her second ball, which she hit higher and harder than the first one. She whooped with delight.

Mike's second ball flew straight out and way high.

Her third ball went even farther.

"You hit pretty hard there," Mike said, whacking his third ball the farthest of all.

"Not as hard as you."

"We can see how close we came tomorrow. Maybe after work?"

"Great." She stared out to where the balls had gone. That had been fun and satisfying and it did make her feel less frustrated. She turned to say so to Mike and—

His mouth was right there, his hand at her cheek, and he kissed her. It was great—urgent and gentle, lips and tongue at once, teasing and hungry at the same time. She wanted it to go on and on. She was sinking into him and flying away at the same time, lighter than air, riding one of Jasmine's pink clouds.

Then, Mike broke it off.

"Why did you do that?" she gasped.

"I got carried away."

"No. I mean why did you stop?"

"I'm your boss, Autumn," he said.

"Not until tomorrow, you're not."

She leaned in, but he backed up. "It was inappropriate. I don't know what's wrong with me."

"Nothing's wrong with you. Or me, either. We have an intense attraction."

"Like my brother and your friend. Yeah."

And they certainly didn't want to go *there*. That was his message and she agreed with all her heart.

Her pink cloud evaporated instantly and Autumn hit the ground hard. She'd been ready to have sex on a dead and dusty golf green. Way too weird.

"I really apologize," Mike said, looking so guilty.

"We kissed, okay? Don't go painting a scarlet A on your forehead, Mike."

"Still. I was way out of line."

"What? Mayors are superhuman now?"

"Got the cape and tights in the trunk." He smiled, but he clearly still felt awful.

"Leave them there. You're fine. I'm fine. It's okay." But she was aware that her heart was still pounding from the kiss. "We should head back. I need sleep to impress my new boss tomorrow."

"Ouch." He grimaced.

She put a hand on his arm. "Don't do that. I wanted you to kiss me."

"Yeah?"

"Oh, yeah." But he was right to stop. She had an internship to focus on. She needed her feet planted firmly on the shore, not flailing around in the deep end of an unpredictable sea.

They were quiet for the short drive. Through the sunroof Autumn watched the moon follow them home. Now and then she turned to smile reassuringly at Mike. *No harm done.*

Back in town, Mike parked beside her car in the high school parking lot and helped her out, hanging on to her hand for a few extra seconds. "I'll see you in the morning?" His eyes held regret. He'd wanted more. Good. It was no fun wishing for more all alone.

"Bright and early. You bet."

"Not early. You'll upset Evelyn. She'll think you're trying to show her up."

"Okay. On time then." She looked around the quiet streets. There were no cars moving and barely any lights—just a few security bulbs inside business and the tall lights in the school lot where they stood. "I guess it's good no one's around," she said. "Being out alone so late together...talk about starting gossip."

"Yeah." He smiled ruefully, then looked past her and

his smile fell away. "Speaking of which…that's my brother's car."

She turned and saw something move across the rear window of the Acura sedan—an arm, then a head. A familiar head. Jasmine and Mark were making out in the backseat. "Wow."

"Yeah. Wow," he said grimly.

They'd been so crazed they couldn't make it to a house. What would that be like? Thrilling and scary, like the deep end of the pool she'd nearly slipped into with Mike.

I want that. She felt it so fiercely she had to brace herself against her bumper.

"So do we leave them here?" Mike asked.

"If someone else sees, they'd be mortified."

"Yeah." Mike sighed. "I'll send them home. Unless you think you can sleep through that?" He nodded at the rocking car.

"If I have to, I could."

"I know what you mean." His eyes held heat. He didn't want to have to listen to Mark and Jasmine doing what they wanted to be doing any more than she did.

"Got a coin?" she asked him.

"Huh?" He fished out a quarter.

"You flip and I'll call."

He smiled, braced it on his thumb and tossed it upward.

"Heads," she said, and they held each other's gaze while the quarter flew and spun up, then down.

Mike caught it without looking and slapped it onto the back of his hand. *Tails* shone up at them. "Looks like I'm the lucky one."

"Sorry."

"Get some sleep." He touched her cheek, looking bewildered. "I don't know what came over me."

"Oh, I do." It was lust, pure and simple, stoked by the hours together, how comfortable they'd been, everything they'd shared. They'd slipped easily into a teasing flirtation and just gone too far. "Blame it on the desert, the night, the stars. Hell, blame it on golf."

"If you say so." He backed away, still watching her, then raised a hand in farewell before turning to lope to the car to tell the couple where they would be banging the headboard.

She stood for a second, trying to shake off the spell. Out there at the resort, she'd forgotten who she was, what she wanted, everything but the warm man whose lips were on hers.

She realized she wasn't scared to go to work now.

Which caused a cold thought to trickle through her brain. What if the flirtation had been about the job? What if she'd worked the physical attraction because the mental challenge scared her? After all, if her boss was attracted to her, he'd have to keep her on. Had that been her unconscious trick? It was second nature to use sex appeal to get what she wanted.

But that was unacceptable. The new Autumn was better than that. Smarter, too. And tomorrow she'd prove it.

5

AFTER A SLEEPLESS NIGHT, Mike's brain was full of white noise and his eyelids felt coated with sandpaper. At first Mark and Jasmine kept him awake, going at it as though they'd invented the act. A down pillow over his head hadn't blocked the moans and shrieks and thuds.

But after that it was all about Autumn. He'd enjoyed her company so much. The hours had flown by, which was odd, since he usually tracked every tick of time.

Then he'd lost all sense and kissed her.

He was her employer, for God's sake. Wasn't it bad enough that he'd hired her out of guilt over ogling her? He had no idea whether she could even do the job. References notwithstanding, she was a student and Lydia's system was not simple.

He'd hired her anyway. And then he'd kissed her.

Talking with her, laughing, teasing her, he'd realized how lonely he'd been, as empty and lost as that deserted resort. Standing there under a starry sky, he'd wanted to taste her, hold her, sink deep into her lush body.

What was his problem? He'd had plenty of feminine company over the past six months. He'd dated four women and slept with two. Attractive, intelligent, professional women.

He'd enjoyed them.

But he didn't long for them.

Autumn Beshkin was the kind of woman a man craved. He'd always wanted that.

Something about her…an air of mystery and secret depths, a knowing cynicism with an edge of hope. She reminded him of the season she'd been named for, with its changing light, golden moon, crisp air and nature splashing the trees gold, rust and red. Autumn.

Hell, she'd turned him into a poet.

He couldn't believe he'd told her he wanted to be a pilot. She'd been so eager about her new life that he'd flashed on the road not taken, the things he'd pushed down, shrugged off, ignored. Her excitement made him grin, made him kiss her.

It was crazy. Chemistry. As fleeting as sparks from a campfire. What he wanted was a relationship, making a life with someone, working through problems, setting goals and achieving them. At thirty-five, he was too old to think with his parts.

Still, there was something about Autumn. She was smart and funny and original, of course, but something else got to him—the way she came on strong, chin up. One tough cookie who expected to elbow her way to what she'd earned, by God, as if she didn't dare hope for things to work out. Which hit him in the heart, made him want to bulldoze a clear path for her. Made him want to make her happy.

Jesus, Mike, you just met her.

But she was so…*unusual.* Unpredictable. Ferocious and shaky at the same time. And he couldn't wait to see her again.

He dragged himself out of bed, got ready and

headed in to work. He loved his drive into town. Right away, he picked up the sweet tang of prickly pear jelly stewing in the Cactus Confections vats.

The factory was located in one of three historic buildings, including a defunct blacksmith shop and what passed for a museum housed in the old post office/assay office. Sally's Knit Hut now inhabited the old mercantile. There were federal monies available for the restoration of historic districts if he could only carve out the time to write the grant proposals.

At the town limits, Ned Langton was planting the flowers in the Welcome to Copper Corners sign. True to his word, he seemed to be almost ready for the Founder's Day dedication.

Turning the corner, Mike watched Jeff Randolph swipe his neighbor's *Copper Corners Dispatch*. Jeff refused to pay the carrier over some nonsense about too many tosses in his cholla bed and chose, instead, to irritate his neighbors. Jeff was a jerk, but he'd donated more money than anyone for Darren Goble's reconstructive surgery after the tractor accident.

Mike loved this town and all the people in it, flaws and all. Driving down Main, he felt a renewed sense of mission. The citizens of Copper Corners had faith in him. They'd elected him for a third term, hadn't they?

Not that anyone had expressed any interest in running against him. Not many go-getters in Copper Corners. If you wanted to make a mark, you left town.

Yeah, Copper Corners was small and people gossiped, did petty things, were selfish and sometimes mean. People in cities weren't any better. The difference was that in a small town, like in a family, you solved conflicts, worked around warts and foibles. You didn't give up on each other, get a new job or grab a cab out of town.

Who was he arguing with?

Autumn. She'd tilted her head at him as though he was as quaint as the little town that owned his heart. He had no regrets.

Or very few, anyway.

He passed the high school, the elementary school, the pizzeria and the downtown shops, then pulled into the town hall lot and parked in the mayor spot—not that he ever had to fight for space. Especially not this early in the morning.

He was surprised to see Evelyn's blue Toyota Camry with its license plate border painted like lace. Autumn's car—a silver Subaru WR X, sexy and practical, like the woman herself—wasn't there yet.

Inside, Evelyn held the phone between her ear and shoulder while she knitted what looked to be a baby blanket. Already, Lydia and Bud must have Evelyn's fluffy handiworks bursting out their windows and doors.

When she saw him, Evelyn stopped sewing and dropped her jaw. "Hang on," she said to her caller. "You getting an award somewhere, Mayor Mike?"

"Of course not," he said, feigning innocence.

"Dress slacks and a tie? And is that shirt ironed?"

"So?"

"You should see him, Karen," she said into the phone. She was talking to her daughter, Mike knew. She leaned across her desk and sniffed at him. "That a cologne sample from *GQ?*" Quincy sneezed and shook himself before bounding off the desk, as if he'd gotten too big a whiff, as well.

"Heidi gave me the stuff for Christmas. Thought I should get some use out of it." He shrugged. "You finished on the phone?" He didn't care to participate in third-party abuse.

"Oh, yeah. Just a sec." She lowered her mouth to the phone. "Karen, honey, I'll come see Kimmie give her speech… Yeah… Bye." She set down the phone and honed in on him—no mercy in her gaze. "I don't guess your new look and smell has anything to do with our new employee, does it now?"

"Maybe I'm setting a more professional tone. You might consider that yourself." He nodded at her pink tracksuit.

"I work better comfortable," she said. "You want me lean and mean, right? On the balls of my feet." She pretended to bob and weave from her chair. "I'll lose the cap in a bit. I've got a first-thing appointer with Celia."

"I noticed you were early," he said wryly. It would never be because of a town task.

"Celia said you and Autumn had dinner together last night."

"She's new in town. I wanted to be polite."

She grinned, not buying it. "You're human, Mike. She's beautiful. Go for it."

"What you're suggesting falls in the category of sexual harassment, Evelyn." The last thing he needed was Evelyn eagle-eying him when he was around Autumn.

"Harassment's in the eye of the beholder, darlin'."

"How's Kimmie doing?" Mike asked to change the subject. Evelyn's granddaughter needed minor surgery after a volleyball injury because of the delay getting to Tucson for X-rays. Dr. Coleman's twice-a-month clinics weren't enough for the town.

"Much better. Karen says she's playing normal. Giving a big speech today at school. I'm going, if that's okay? I'll get Autumn to cover the phones."

"Don't overwhelm her now." There was no point arguing with Evelyn and he knew the phones were simple enough. He'd covered them a time or two himself when Evelyn got in a bind. He headed for the bathroom to rinse off the cologne. Maybe he'd primped for his temp, but there was no need to make people's eyes water.

The bathroom door jingled when he opened it. Evelyn had decorated everything, including the inside handle. The silk flower pot had a crocheted cover, she'd shellacked the toilet seat with pictures of lucky items—horseshoes, aces and rabbit feet. And a rack of shelves held hand-painted ceramic items—gnomes and deer and chipmunks and whatnot. If only he could harness her talent for good, instead of kitsch.

He'd get her to coordinate the craft booths for the Founder's Day festival. Sure. Pleased, he grabbed a paper towel.

He was scrubbing his neck when the door flew open, thumping him on the back of the head so he bumped his forehead on the mirror over the sink.

Rubbing the spot, he turned to find Autumn standing there, eyes wide with concern. "Oh. I'm sorry, Mike."

"No problem." He stopped rubbing when he noticed a big blotch on the white blouse that peeked from her dark jacket—coffee from the Gas-N-Go cup she held, he figured.

Her outfit was so tight it looked sprayed on and gave him an ache behind the designer belt Heidi had given him.

"I spilled," she said, touching the smear on her chest. He backed up to let her in. They stood inches apart, since Evelyn's crafts made the room as cramped as a jet john.

Just a few hours ago, he'd tasted her lips, heard her ragged breathing, seen the fire in her green eyes. He froze, not sure what to do or even how to feel.

She sniffed in the direction of his neck. "M7, huh?" Her voice had a sexy, teasing lilt that relieved him. It meant they'd moved beyond the unbearable lust of the night before and were back to relaxed flirting.

"I went too heavy, Evelyn tells me." He reached past her to toss the paper towel in the trash, enjoying the chance to inhale her fresh and spicy perfume.

"Easy to do with the high-end stuff."

"I'll remember next time. Thanks."

"Any time. Got any tips for getting coffee out of silk?" Her fingers fluttered at her cleavage.

"Not really." *But I'd love to watch you try.* What had she worn under this blouse? It was white, so not black leather—it would show. What about stockings? He didn't dare look down. *Stop it.* He was drowning in testosterone, as well as M7.

"You look nice, too," she said. "Different from yesterday."

"I thought I should…I mean…yeah." He flushed. She knew he'd dressed up for her. Like a hick.

"It's okay, Mike. We can joke around, right? I mean, last night was last night and today is today?" There was a flicker of uncertainty in her words that told him that she felt last night on her skin, too, tasted it on her lips. Her solution was to brazen it out. Not a bad idea.

"Sure. I'll get out of your way," he said in a businesslike tone, backing out of the room. "When you're through, I'll set you up in Lydia's office."

A few minutes later, he looked up from festival planning to find her leaning against his doorjamb looking sexier than ever. What the…? With a jolt, he realized she'd taken off her blouse, revealing a wedge of creamy flesh between her lapels, which were held together by one measly button. And it looked damn loose. A flick of a finger and there she'd be. Nearly naked.

Mortified by his thoughts, he walked toward her, a file held strategically at groin level. "Lydia's office is there." He gestured and she preceded him into the windowless space.

"It used to be a supply closet, but Lydia needs quiet to work and Evelyn lives to chat. Sorry there's no window."

"I hardly need a view. I'm only here for a month."

"Have a seat," he said, noticing Lydia's desk was piled with unopened mail, her inbox stacked with invoices and purchase orders. Monthly budget reports had been due last week.

"We got a little behind because Lydia left so quickly." Page Wiley, the clerk, had made the daily deposits but hadn't reconciled, and stacks of tax assessments had to be handled.

"That's why you have me. To catch you up and maybe get you ahead."

He squatted to click on her computer tower, putting them eye to eye. "I'm glad you're here," he said, despite the fact he didn't know for sure that she could handle the job.

"Me, too." She smiled, then turned to the monitor. "I'll need a password to log in?"

"Ah, right." He stood. "Lydia put together some instructions." In the upright rack, he found a purple folder labeled For Temp and handed it to her.

She opened the folder. "Log-in info right on top. Also, her voice mail pass code. And I'll read through the rest of this." She waved the folder at him, suggesting he let her get to it.

"So, anything else you need?" He straightened the stack in Lydia's inbox.

"Any priorities?"

"Catch up with invoices and billings, record the tax assessments, make the deposits and mail out the receipts. That's daily." He studied her. "I don't know Lydia's system. The town clerk, Page Wiley, might know a little more."

"A spreadsheet is a spreadsheet. Don't worry." She smiled a tight smile. "Her system is probably an adaptation of a program I know."

"Lydia's in the online address book. Lydia Bennington. She said to call if we need help."

"I'll be fine."

Would she even admit it if she wasn't? "One more thing. We're running late on our budget cycle. When you get ahead a bit, I need you to consolidate the proposed budgets I've gotten with what Lydia has already. I'd like to present them to the council on Thursday."

"I'll get right on that then." She bent to adjust the chair's height.

He shut his eyes against seeing her cleavage.

"Mike?"

When he opened his eyes, she was looking at him curiously. "You okay?"

"Uh, yeah. Fine. If you have questions, ask." He backed away. "Not that I'll be of much help, but—" He bumped into the door. "I'd like to go over the budgets this afternoon."

"Sure. No problem." But she bit her lip, worried.

He busied himself contacting the festival committee chairs. He had to talk Ned Langton out of his signature game—Cow Pie Tic-Tac-Toe. How the hell could Mike bring the town into the twenty-first century when the most popular game focused on where a cow chose to drop her load?

As he worked, he worried about how Autumn was doing. He hoped she was up to the job. He'd kissed the woman. He sure as hell didn't want to have to fire her.

DO THE HARD PART first. That always worked best, Autumn knew, so she ignored the stack of mail, the invoices and billings and clicked into the accounting program. These were most of Lydia's working files— tax assessments, utility billings, fines and fees, police confiscation inventory and tons more. This was far more complex than bookkeeping for a strip club. Her stomach tightened and sweat popped out all over her body. *You can do it. You have to.*

First, she clicked into the tax assessment file, hoping it would look familiar. Nope. Not a bit like any spreadsheet she'd worked with. Her heart sank. The purple folder contained instructions on day-to-day procedures and the shelves held no software manuals or notebooks.

Okay, do a save-as and experiment. Except the file was huge and in the middle of the save the computer froze. Damn. She hard-started the machine, praying she hadn't corrupted the file.

"Everything okay?" Mike stuck his head in the door while the machine ground away, sounding in pain. She half expected smoke to rise.

"Just getting started. Fine so far," she said breezily. God, what if she killed the computer? A good accountant was supposed to cut costs not incur them.

"Let me know if you need anything," he said.

"I'm just fine," she sang. She would be, dammit. She'd figure this out if it killed her. And if the system didn't load, she just might have to kill herself. Hang herself by her mouse cord, cut her wrists with a mechanical pencil, something.

As soon as Mike left, though, the log-on screen popped up and the low hum of a working computer filled the air. No smoke. Whew. She couldn't make a practice copy, so now what?

Learn by doing. Okay. She would enter a tax payment. She keyed the numbers into the relevant columns, hit what she thought was the "calculate" key and got error symbols. Damn. "Backspace" condensed the cells and she couldn't get them to toggle back. Double damn.

Five minutes into her first job and she was DOA. Now what? Mike couldn't help and she didn't want to alarm the town clerk she hadn't met. Her chest felt so tight she could hardly breathe. She wanted to crawl out of her sweat-slick skin. She'd have to call Lydia. What else could she do? She'd pretend she just wanted to touch base, introduce herself, go over the notes. Yeah. That sounded good.

Pulling her confidence around her like a costume, she found and dialed the number. She would be cool, ease into her questions, be casual and professional.

Lydia's phone rang and rang and rang. When the machine finally kicked in, Autumn left a breezy message that ended, "If you get a chance, when it's convenient, if you could buzz me back." Between the lines, Lydia couldn't miss her true message: *Save me. I'm in deep weeds.*

Autumn turned back to the computer. In her panic, the numbers seemed to smear before her eyes. So what if she'd been a good student? This was the real world, where it counted. She couldn't fail here. Or quit.

She'd done a lot of quitting over the years. She'd quit the work-study program she'd been enrolled in before she started stripping because it seemed too hard. Before that she'd walked out on the GED exam. There were other times, such as when she'd chickened out on the dance troupe audition. There were always reasons, but she felt like a quitter.

Now she felt faint, so she put her head between her knees, fighting for calm. In her mind, she suddenly saw Quincy with that reassuring look on his face. She almost wanted to grab that big, fat, *particular* cat and bury her nose in his fur.

That made her smile and calmed her down. She sat up. *It's a spreadsheet, not a nuclear bomb.*

While she waited for Lydia to call back, she would organize the mail. Digging into envelopes with the letter opener eased her tension and before long she remembered the Excel files on her jump drive. She could use one of those spreadsheets and export the data later, after she figured out the custom software.

Use what you got. She knew that. Thinking of Quincy helped her remember.

Before long, Evelyn returned and stuck her head into Autumn's office, bringing a wave of hairspray with her. "What do you think?" She turned her head, fluffing her new do.

"Very nice, Evelyn. You look younger."

"She got the bangs too short. We got to analyzing my daughter Karen's marriage and Celia went a little far with the scissors." She shrugged. "It'll grow. You doing okay?"

"Fine, I think. Though I had a little trouble with—"

"Good, cuz I'm gonna forward the phone and take an early lunch. My granddaughter Kimmie's giving a speech at the high school. People know to ding the call bell out front."

"Okay, but I—"

"There's tea and coffee in the kitchen. Cookies, too, but I don't recommend them. I'm not sure Kimmie understood what *sift ingredients* means. Every bite's a surprise—flour, bitter chocolate, baking powder, you never know."

Evelyn left and Autumn kept working. Page Wiley helped her figure out the details for paychecks, which Autumn would prepare for Friday. Answering the phone, she talked to most of the dozen town employees who worked in the office complex next door. They all asked her how she liked the town, how Mike was treating her, as if they had all the time in the world to chat. Maybe they did. Small towns. She, on the other hand, had to get the budget stuff ready for Mike this afternoon.

Whenever she sent him a call, her heart revved up. They had their attraction under control, at least. She'd felt comfortable enough to flirt with him a little, which relieved the tension and felt…safe.

At 11:30, the front bell jangled and she heard Jasmine call her name.

"Back here," she replied, happy to see her friend, who bustled in eagerly.

"Look at you!" she said, looking around the space. "Your own office, your own desk, your own computer." She paused at a painting of a crying clown. "Even your own bad art. Doesn't that make you feel great?"

Autumn paused and let the idea sink in. "Yeah. It does actually." She was on her way, really, toward the future she longed for. If only Lydia would call her back, she'd feel better.

"You look so professional and formal with your hair like that, wearing a suit."

"Good." Having every hair in place, a sharp suit and dress pumps seemed crucial to her. Business dress led to a business attitude, which led to business success. All part of the package. "What are you up to?" Autumn nodded at the three-ring binder in Jasmine's arms.

"Sketching costumes, getting my shopping list for Tucson—fabrics and trims and all. I want to take you to lunch to make up for last night's dinner. I mean, I wanted us to have some fun together."

"You're not meeting Mark?"

"He had to show some houses. We'll have time tonight. Sheila has a commitment so rehearsal is short and early." She sighed. "I miss him so much when we're apart, it's ridiculous."

"Just don't get so carried away that you—"

"Get naked in the school parking lot? Yeah. We just couldn't stop, you know. I've never felt like this before."

Jasmine never remembered how bad it got. "You said the same thing about Ricardo, remember? And Tyson before that."

Jasmine held up her hands. "Do not rain on my

sunny day, Autumn Beshkin. It was wishful thinking with Ricardo. And Tyson was a rebound thing. This is different."

Jasmine put her heart on the line every time. "Recovery is agony, Jasmine, remember? I just don't want—"

"I'll be fine, Autumn. I mean it. This is—"

"Different. You told me. Take your time. Don't do anything rash. These things tend to—" *end badly* "—get complicated," she finished in deference to Jasmine's hope-bright face.

"Oh, I know. We have lots to work out, but, that's the thing. We know we can do it. What's between us is solid."

The front door clanged, Autumn heard fast footsteps, then Mark appeared, windblown and eager. "Jasmine!" he said. "I had a cancellation." He made it sound as if he'd just returned from war.

"You did?" She seemed thrilled, then her face sank. "Oh. But I made plans…" She turned to Autumn.

"Go ahead," Autumn said. "Have lunch together. I can't leave this minute anyway. Evelyn's not back."

"No, that's not right," Jasmine said firmly. "I'm taking you to lunch. Friendship matters. I'll put on some lipstick."

Mike had stepped out of his office and leaned against the wall, ankles crossed. He shook his head at Autumn over the lunch-crossed lovers.

Mark followed Jasmine down the hall, shrugging at Mike when he passed him.

"So, how are things going?" Mike said, pushing away from the door.

"Great," she fibbed, meeting him halfway, so he couldn't look over her shoulder at her computer mess.

"I e-mailed you the budget template and the budgets I have."

"I found a couple of handwritten ones in Lydia's folder. One from a Dave Williams? The other has to do with roads, but I couldn't read the signature."

"Dave is our public works guy. The illegible name is Rick Berber—roads manager. Those two hate computers. See if you can type what they sketched out into the template I attached."

"I'm on it." She only hoped she would be.

"Think we can go over it by the end of the day?"

"Of course." More wild promises.

"You're jumping in with both feet, Autumn. That's great. Even covering for Evelyn. She still out?"

She nodded. "I'm glad to help." If Lydia would just call…

She became aware of a bumping sound coming from down the hall behind Mike. "What is that?" A distinct moan reached them and the bumping got more rhythmic.

"Exactly what you think it is," Mike said. "A nooner." He checked his watch. "Half an hour early."

"Sheesh." She felt hot all over with Mike standing so close. Jasmine cried out. Mark groaned.

"Those two never stop, do they?" Autumn whispered.

"You should have heard them last night."

"Did you get any sleep at all?" The banging got louder. Her body had gone tight and warm as she listened.

"Not much," Mike said. "But it wasn't all because of them." His gaze softened.

"I know what you mean. I was awake awhile, too."

"Yeah. Last night was—"

From down the hall, there was a rattle, followed by a smashing sound. Mike grinned. "Sounds like one of Evelyn's gnomes bit the dust. Unfortunately, she'll make more."

"I'm sorry to hear that." They were smiling at each other when the front door jangled and Evelyn called out, "Hey, kids. What's happening?"

"Uh, nothing," Mike said, moving in her direction, trying to head her off from the hall action. "How did Kimmie do?"

"I am so proud of her. Takes after her Grams, no question."

From down the hall came a shriek.

"Heavenly lord, what was that?" Evelyn hurried that way.

"Nothing. Really," Autumn said, trying to prevent Evelyn from bursting in on the nooner, but the woman was lightning on Nikes and she reached the bathroom door just as it flew open.

"There's a mouse!" Jasmine pointed into the room.

They all crowded around to see Mark pounding here and there with the crochet-decorated tissue box.

"Stop that. You're getting it dusty." Evelyn yanked the tissue box away from him, then brushed it off. "That overstuffed fuzz ball Quincy is supposed to be this great mouser and he hasn't caught one darn rodent."

Then Evelyn noticed the smashed tchotchke on the floor. "My chipmunk." She picked up the piece of striped back and shot Mark a forlorn and accusatory look.

"Sorry." He shrugged.

"I'll have to finish my squirrel and bring it in." She reverently gathered up the pieces and carried them out.

When she was gone, Mark gave Jasmine a quick peck and whispered, "See you tonight," then shot an apologetic look toward Autumn and Mike before he took off.

"Let's go eat," Jasmine said to Autumn. "I'm starving."

"Worked up an appetite chasing the mouse, huh?" Mike asked, winking at Autumn. She felt a warm connection with him, a bond. "See you in a bit," he said.

"Yeah," she said, only hoping she'd get everything he needed done on time.

6

"SO WHAT'S WITH THE MAYOR?" Jasmine said, leaning forward. "Was he mad at you for taking a lunch? He stared at you all the way out the door."

"No. Not at all," she said. "Not yet, anyway." It was nice to know he couldn't take his eyes off her, though. She tapped her nails nervously on the table, thinking about all she had to do.

"Look, you lost your nail decal," Jasmine said. "Your birthday design, right?"

"Shoot." She studied the index nail. She'd had Esmeralda reapply the star design twice since April when her friend created it for their birthday celebration. Autumn's frantic typing must have knocked off the stone and the stenciled polish.

"I hope that's not a bad sign," Autumn said. That comment sounded like Esmeralda, who not only did nails, but read palms and tea leaves and auras and whatever else she could get her hands on. The birthday she shared with Esmeralda and their friend Sugar always included a nail design and an Esmeralda reading.

"What did your psychic friend predict again?" Jasmine asked.

"Oh, I don't know. *Big changes in head and hearth and heart.* Whatever that means." She shrugged. She didn't buy that psychic jazz. Her future wasn't written in pekoe dregs. It was hers to create. She studied her sadly plain finger, though, wishing the Cut 'N Curl had a nail tech who could reproduce the design.

"Wait," Jasmine said, excited. "Let's see. You've got a job." She ticked a finger. "That's *head*. And you're living here. That's a change in *hearth*." Another tick. "Wow. All you need is your heart. Maybe you'll fall in love in Copper Corners. What about that?"

"Insane," she said quickly, shifting on the bench, not wanting her friend to come up with Mike as a possibility. "Try the machaca burritos, Jas. I hear they're the best." When Jasmine began to study the menu, Autumn breathed out in relief.

And heart would lead. That's also what Esmie had said. Ridiculous, Autumn thought. Except that Esmie's prediction for Sugar had come true, after all, when she fell in love with her business partner not three weeks after the reading. It had shocked Autumn, since she and Sugar had shared the belief that a long-time love wasn't for either of them.

Very strange. Esmie's final warning to Autumn, complete with wagging finger had been, *Don't kick your heart to the curb.*

"Ooh, look. They make prickly pear margaritas," Jasmine said, looking up at her. "Isn't that your favorite?"

It was the traditional birthday drink, actually.

"It says Cactus Confections produces the mix and ships it all over the world. You probably had a little taste of Copper Corners yourself. Want one?"

"No thanks. I have work."

"Me, too. I'll have to settle for prickly pear iced tea." Suze took their orders and Jasmine continued her Mark

Fields Rhapsody in Lust. "We are just so compatible. I mean, we never stop talking."

"Oh, yeah, you do."

Jasmine giggled. "Well, *that*. But, honestly, we talk more than we screw. And Mark's thinking of moving to Phoenix."

"But I thought you weren't going to be rash."

"When you know it's right, you know."

"He's in real estate. How can he move like *that?*" Autumn snapped her fingers.

"You do what you have to do." Jasmine shrugged.

Autumn went for a new tack. "Have you thought about Sabrina? How this will affect her?"

"Sabrina is my breath, my sun and stars, Autumn. Of course I've thought about her. Your advice is great— I *need* your advice, I do—but don't treat me like I can't cross the street alone."

"I'm sorry. I just don't want—"

"Me to get hurt. Got it. I'm taking Mark to Cactus Ranch on visiting day to get Sabrina's approval."

"Maybe you should see how this goes after you get back to Phoenix, huh? If you're still together, then introduce her."

Jasmine steadied her gaze on Autumn's face. "You think I'm going to blow this, don't you?"

"It's not that. Mark's never met a woman like you. And men who are thinking with their—who aren't thinking clearly—don't always make good decisions." She wouldn't mention the real estate con artist Mike had told her about. Not yet, anyway. "You come from different worlds, Jas."

"Love makes all things possible."

Autumn gritted her teeth and fought a groan. "Not all

things. Get the kinks worked out before you involve Sabrina, okay? Do that for me. For Auntie Autumn, huh?"

"Look, I'm not taking this personal because I know you're projecting your own fears on me, but really—"

"Projecting my own what?"

"You assume I feel the way you would feel. That's projection. But I'm not you. I'm not afraid of love like you."

"I'm not afraid of love."

"Then why are you never in it?"

"Because I don't—want it." Jasmine, with her wretched history, should understand. But in that way she was like the fish in the Huffmans' tank—the plastic castle was a surprise every time. Maybe most humans had amnesia about the pain of heartbreak. Autumn sure didn't.

Jasmine grabbed her hand. "Don't worry. Love will come to you when you're ready. I'm just ready now."

"Whatever you say." If it were possible to truly be with someone, to trust him—and herself—Autumn might be interested. In reality, it just seemed too good to be true. She stuck with what she trusted, what she understood—sex, not love. Love she didn't get at all. And here was Jasmine sinking into the black hole of it, not even holding out a hand for Autumn to drag her to safety. It was too depressing for words.

Autumn headed back to the town hall after lunch just in time for more bad news. Evelyn was gone again, leaving her a note she had to tug from beneath Quincy, who gave her the feline evil eye.

Evelyn's scrawl read, *Gone to Tucson to see Lydia and Bud's baby! Darwin Baldwin Smysor, born ll:32 a.m., St. Joseph's Hospital, twenty-two inches, seven pounds and perfect! Hooray!*

Autumn was happy for Lydia, of course, but no way

would a brand-new mother chit-chat about spread-sheets and inputs. She probably hadn't even gotten Autumn's call. Autumn felt acid eat away at her stomach. She would just have to try her Excel ad-lib.

Mike must have heard her come in and he stepped out of his office, holding a folder. "Good lunch?"

"More or less." She didn't have the heart to mention Mark's plan to move. Mike would hear soon enough, she was sure. "So, Lydia had her baby?" She waved the note.

"Yeah. I sent flowers. I'll go after work to see them."

"That's sweet of you."

He shrugged. "Lydia's like family. That's how it is in small towns."

"I can see that." The idea had a certain amount of appeal, the way the world of a fairy tale seemed so quaint and darling.

"When you get a chance, cut these checks for deposits on the festival booths and equipment, please." He handed her a folder. "And can we meet at four on the budgets? Normally I work late, but I want to get out to see Lydia."

"Sure. No problem." Her heart lurched at all the promises she was making that she wasn't sure she could fulfill.

"That'd be great."

She turned to go.

"Autumn?" he called softly.

She turned to him.

"It's a weight off my mind to have good help."

"I'm glad." The acid in her stomach lapped higher.

"Holler if you have any holes you need me to fill in." *How about in my stomach? Got Maalox?* "You bet."

Back in her office, she readied the checks for his signature, then dug into the budget e-mail Mike had sent. It had seven department budgets and the line item adjustments he'd made. Unable to merge the tables, she copied and pasted each entry, afraid to check the time ticking by so fast.

Her back ached and her eyes burned, but at five to four, when Mike popped his head in, she'd just highlighted everything to change to a better typeface before she printed it all out.

"You all set? It go okay?"

"No sweat," she lied, her neck aching from the strain. "I'll print it and we can go over it." Showing off, she whipped around, flicked the save shortcut keys, then select all then print. At first, she thought she'd hit something wrong, but the printer in the hall hummed, so she knew she'd done fine.

Mike waited for her in the door to her office. "This is great. I'll be able to get to the hospital before supper. I usually don't get out of here before seven."

"No wonder you don't have a social life." She became aware how quiet the building was. Evelyn had gone to see the baby. Most town employees ended their shifts at four, so the adjoining offices were mostly empty, too.

"I try to keep weekends down to a few hours." Mike's voice had gone low, as if he, too, realized they were alone and the pull between them rose again, crackling with electricity.

"Anything I can do to give you a life, Mayor Mike," she said, running a finger along the lapel of her jacket. Cocky with success, she felt free to tease, knowing she was safe. They'd agreed that last night was last night, but a little flirting could be fun.

Mike's gaze followed her finger, then jerked up. He

cleared his throat. "You, um, get the stain out of your blouse?" He nodded at where the white silk blouse hung from the hook on the back of her door.

"Not quite." She fingered the fabric. "I'll have to try stain remover. This blouse cost a fortune."

"Looks it," he murmured, catching her gaze. "We're usually pretty casual around here. Especially in summer."

"Except for today." She nodded at his pressed shirt. He'd undone his tie and it hung loose and sexy down both sides of the starched surface.

He flushed. "I was trying to impress you."

"Consider me impressed." Their eyes locked like heat-seeking missiles dead on target.

Autumn's pulse pounded in her head and a tiny quiver started up deep within her. She pushed a strand of hair into her braid, then grimaced from the scalp tightness.

"Something hurt?"

"My scalp gets sore from the pull of my braid."

"So take it down."

"Now?"

"Why not?"

There was a challenge in his words, so she reached back, pulled the pins that held the ends in place, separated the strands and shook out her hair.

Mike watched, his eyes following the sway of her hair. "Better?"

"Much."

"Yeah. Better." His eyes dipped to her breasts, then to the button on her jacket, which she circled with a finger.

"You with me?" she teased with a slow smile.

He dragged his eyes up. "Sorry. This is bad. We're at work. I'm your boss. All that."

"True. But after last night, things are different. We're having fun."

"You call this fun? You took off your blouse," he breathed.

"It seemed sensible." She flicked at the button with her nail.

"Careful." He gave a slow grin. "After yesterday, though, I have to say I'm curious about what's underneath."

"After yesterday?"

"When we were fighting over your binder, you leaned down and I happened to see…"

"Ah. My bra." Her Leather Girl costume. With open nipples. The thought sent a charge through her like lightning. No wonder he'd looked so pole-axed for a few seconds there.

"And did you like it?" she teased.

He nodded slowly. "Oh, yeah. Not to mention the, uh, stockings. Under your suit, you were dressed for…"

"Something more fun?" she said, giving him a wicked smile, glad he didn't know her secret—she'd been dressed to strip. "So when you offered me the job, you were thinking about my underwear?"

"Not exactly, no, but, it was in my mind. I'm not proud of that. It's not like me to be so—"

"Male?" She laughed lightly, liking how open-hearted he was being, so honest. "Relax, Mike. I noticed your reaction and I pushed it."

"Really?" He seemed relieved.

"Really. For me to be upset you'd have to have done something I didn't like." She spoke low and slow.

"And you liked me staring at you? Wanting you?" His dark eyes drew her nearer.

"Not very professional, huh?" The idea of using his attraction had upset Autumn yesterday. Today, it was a relief to joke about it. Mike made it easy somehow.

"Nor for me. I'm the mayor, remember? Your boss?" He shifted just slightly closer, heating the moment even more. Lust swelled and subsided in his eyes, like an ocean wave washing to shore, then pulling back, only to return again for more.

"Peach silk," she finally breathed.

"Excuse me?"

"My bra today. Edged in white lace." Her baby-doll slumber party costume. Her words registered in his face. Every sexy thing she said got to him and that made her feel so powerful.

"You're pushing it again, aren't you?"

In answer, she whispered, "And my panties match."

He groaned as if her words caused him pain.

She shivered with the thrill of the moment. This was so hot. Because it was forbidden. Because Mike was so respectable. Because she'd thrown him.

But she was at work, doing a job that was important to both of them. "Let me show you what I've got," she said, striving for a businesslike tone.

"Can't wait," he said.

"My work, not my underwear." She was still smiling when she looked at what she'd printed. Except instead of ten pages, she had a single page with "fg" at the top. "Wait. What happened? Hang on."

Freaked, she raced back to her office and found her computer screen blank except for "fg." "Oh, my God."

"What's wrong?" Mike had joined her.

"I bumped some keys." She'd highlighted the entire document, then hit *f* and *g*, replacing the entire report with those two stupid letters. She'd been showing off and ruined everything.

Burning with panic, she clicked undo, but nothing changed. It couldn't. She'd overwritten the report and saved the changes. She looked up at him. "I accidentally deleted the whole report. It's gone." She closed her eyes, struggling with the frustration and embarrassment.

"Are you sure?"

"It took me hours and hours." Her neck was still cramped from the repetitive commands.

"I distracted you."

"That's no excuse." She got up from her desk and faced him. "I can come in early and redo it, so we can go over it by noon, maybe sooner. Will that be okay? You need it for Thursday, right?"

"I'll be in Tucson tomorrow, so I don't see how that'll work." He frowned.

"So I'll stay late tonight and bring it to you before you leave? How's that?" She was grasping at straws, she knew.

"No. Go ahead and work on it tomorrow. I'll try to get back early enough to go over it." She could tell he wasn't pleased.

"I'm so sorry. I'll do whatever it takes to fix this."

"It's your first day, Autumn. You're fine." He squeezed her shoulders, trying to tell her he had faith in her.

But she was a fraud, who didn't have a clue how to handle the software she'd promised him would be a breeze. Exhaustion, frustration and self-loathing boiled up in her until, to her horror, she found tears burning her eyes.

"Hey, it's okay. You'll fix it. You're doing great."

"No, I'm not." She brushed her cheeks. "You were right about the software. It's too customized. I'm lost. I even called Lydia this morning. First five minutes on the job and I'm begging for help."

"Lydia expects to help. She'd be happy to talk to you."

"From the hospital?"

"Sure. Well, how about this? When I visit, I'll tell her to give you a call when she's up to it."

"No. She just had a baby, Mike. I'm using one of my spreadsheets and I hope I can upload the data later."

"Look, I'm sure Lydia will want to talk to you."

"If you think she won't mind." She blinked back more tears. Of gratitude this time. She'd folded like a child in front of her first boss in her first real job. "I feel so stupid. I forced you to hire me and now look at me."

"Don't be so hard on yourself," he said. "You know the difference between a P-and-L and an A & P, remember?"

She tried to smile.

"And you're smart and resourceful and you learn fast."

She made one hand into a puppet and pretended to blather. "Blah-blah. That was hire-me hype."

"I have faith in you, Autumn."

"I haven't earned it, but I will, I swear." She meant it. His words were the gift of a friend. She jolted forward to hug him in thanks.

The friendly gesture was a mistake because it sparked instant heat. Mike's fingers pressed into her back, he took a ragged breath and lunged for her mouth. This kiss was not gentle. It was hot and hard and full of need. She kissed him the same way.

He lowered his hands to her bottom and lifted her onto her desk, shoving things out of the way, making room to move. Folders splashed to the floor. Something clanged and began to play "It's a Small, Small World." Lydia's music box.

Autumn leaned back, knocking off the paper clip holder, the springy photo display, something else that clattered.

Mike undid the button on her jacket. "Peach," he said, looking at her bra, "with white lace."

She arched her back, pushing her breasts at him, wanting his hands on her, not caring about anything but him—his mouth, his touch, his desire for her. *Take me. Do me. Screw me now.*

Through the bra, he pressed his lips against her nipple, then roughly tugged down both cups to get at her. He took first one breast, then the other, into his mouth, as if he couldn't choose, couldn't get enough, wanted them both at once.

"Mike," she breathed, lying back on the desk. Her head hit the stapler. "Ouch."

He shoved it away and it fell, along with the clock, and he moved over her. The monitor wobbled, the keyboard hit the floor. She didn't care and neither did he, it seemed.

He reached under her skirt and she grasped him through his pants, going for his zipper so she could touch him, get him inside her. He shoved her skirt up, his palms on her thighs, wanting to get at her. "This is crazy. We're in town hall."

"The door's shut," she breathed. "We're alone."

And then there was a knock.

They froze, stared at each other, dazed and startled.

Caught. Mike helped her off the desk, pulled her jacket together and buttoned it. "You okay?"

She nodded, wobbling.

"Just a moment!" he called, his voice husky. He smoothed her clothes, then adjusted his pants, where his erection was still evident, and headed for the door.

Another knock. More like a thud. Followed by a meow.

"Hell." Mike turned to her, grinning. "It's that damned cat." He opened the door and Quincy strolled in, tail high, acting indignant. "Quincy doesn't like the doors shut."

"Well, la-dee-da," she said, wanting to laugh.

Mike returned to her, eyes twinkling.

They surveyed the half-cleared desk, the mess they'd made of the tiny office. "That was pretty wild," she said.

"Yeah." Mike smoothed her hair away from her face, brushed her cheek with the back of his hand, taking care of her. "I messed you up." He ran his thumb over her lips. "Bruised your lips." ·

"Don't apologize." She bit the pad of his thumb.

His breath hissed in. "Quit that or I'll have us crashing through the walls. They're thin, remember?"

She got the shiver of a wish that he'd do just that. But that was wrong. Poor Mike didn't know what hit him. She understood his lust more than he did and she'd better tamp it down or they'd both be sorry. "I shouldn't have tempted you with my underwear."

"It was more than that. Last night you had me talking about things I let pass by."

And he'd gotten her to babble about how she loved school, why she wanted her own accounting business. She'd felt so comfortable.

"I like having you around," he said.

"I hope you'll still feel that way tomorrow. I'll work on the report in the morning, don't worry."

"I'm not worried," he said, then added softly, "Not about that." Quincy meowed, though what his opinion was, Autumn didn't want to know.

She was worried, too. Their teasing had turned into sex pretty damn fast. It was a little scary.

At home, Autumn found the cats crying for food. Marmalade, as orange as her name, and Mocha, pitch black with thick fur, slid around her legs and she bent to pet them. The fish bobbed to the top of the tank for their flakes. Like an idiot, she said hello. The lizards and turtles had the dignity to ignore her when she refreshed their water and greens.

Restless and unsettled from the incident with Mike, she found a movie on television, then read through the stack of accounting magazines she'd borrowed from her professor.

Still not sleepy, she noticed Jasmine had Sabrina's laptop open on the cocktail table near her research books. Figuring she'd play Solitaire, she sat before the screen.

The browser was open to an article about Arizona history. Looked as though, despite her obsession with Mark, Jasmine had managed to do a little work. Autumn considered that a good sign.

She skimmed the article, reading about how after two gold strikes in 1858 and 1862, the Arizona Territory went from being a barrier to the California gold fields to a strike-it-rich destination of its own.

The article linked to the story of the Copper Strike Mine and its Hanging Tree, where men were hanged for "high-grading," which, from what she gathered, consisted of snitching the biggest nuggets from the ore wagons. She'd noticed the tree by the old flour mill with a brass plaque before it.

Copper Corners' founder Josiah Bremmer was a miner, and shortly after he settled the town, a sect of free thinkers led by Abraham Exeter founded the Common Bread Colony, as a social experiment in communal living, with everyone contributing to the welfare of all with whatever abilities they had— weaving, farming, milling, mining or teaching piano.

Enjoying her reading, Autumn noticed a list of Web sites beside the computer and typed in the address of one that sounded fun—"An Irreverent History of Mining in Southern Arizona."

She'd read some fascinating stuff by the time she heard Jasmine's rattling engine approach around midnight.

Jasmine burst into the house. "Oh, you will not believe what happened, Autumn. We broke the covered wagon."

"You what?"

"Me and Mark. After practice we were just talking and we climbed onto it just to hold each other, you know, but we sort of got busy and the wheels weren't on tight—I mean we were hardly shaking it—and it broke. Can you believe it?"

"You were screwing on a prop, Jasmine, so of course it would break."

"Anyway, the thing was too heavy for us to lift to put back the wheels. We'll just say that we bumped it, I guess." She shrugged, not nearly mortified enough.

On the other hand, who was Autumn to talk? If Quincy hadn't interrupted them, she and Mike would have had sex in town hall. Jasmine's story reminded her how totally insane it had been.

"I can't believe love can be this good," Jasmine said. "It feels like a dream."

"Just be careful, okay?" Autumn said gently. "I mean you can't have sex all over town. It's…indiscreet." Lord, now she was sounding like a tight ass.

"What are you doing awake, anyway?"

"I couldn't sleep."

"Are you nervous about work?"

"I guess." She couldn't tell Jasmine what had happened with Mike. She hardly believed it herself. And talk about losing credibility as Jasmine's sensible advisor. "I was reading the history, thinking it might put me to sleep, but there's interesting stuff here."

"Oh, yeah?"

"Did you know Copper Corners didn't get built because of the mine?"

"It didn't?"

"Get this. It was built around a whore house."

"A what?"

"Or bawdy house, I guess. Yeah. A madam from Chicago inherited a mine claim and came here to check it out and fell in love with Josiah Bremmer and set up shop. The miners came to town to get laid. Evidently, where Cactus Confections is wasn't the Common Bread Colony Communal Hall at all. It was Arizona Rose's Desert Palace, full to the rafters with soiled doves."

She turned the laptop in Jasmine's direction.

Jasmine read for a few seconds, then turned wide eyes to Autumn. "This is so cool. Two people from different worlds fell in love and built a town to celebrate their love. We have to put this in the pageant."

"I doubt the good citizens of Copper Corners want to know their town was founded by hookers." She paused and shared her next thought very gently. "I also think they'll be less than thrilled that the president of the Chamber of Commerce is sleeping with a stripper."

"Exotic dancer, Autumn. And we're burlesque artists now. Why do you have to go for the lowest word?"

"Being a stripper is perfectly respectable."

"Then why do you lie about it?"

"Because it makes things complicated."

"It doesn't have to. Mark is proud of my talent."

He was blinded by desire, but Autumn couldn't say that. "He has a reputation he needs to watch out for."

"Mark is fine with who I am. Your problem is that you don't approve of yourself."

"Please. If you tell me I'm projecting again, I'll make you feed the lizards."

Jasmine shuddered. "Anything but that. Anyway, I'm going to show this stuff to Sheila. Mark and I are going to Tucson tomorrow, by the way. I need fabric and Mark has a real estate thingie. No rehearsal tomorrow night, so we're staying overnight in the city."

"Sounds nice."

"I hate to abandon you. Will you be lonely?"

"I'll manage." With the two of them out of town, at least Mike could get some sleep.

"The other thing is that next Saturday is Family Day at Cactus Ranch. And I'll be taking Mark."

"Do you really want to upset Sabrina at camp?"

"They need to get to know each other."

"Don't pressure her. You know how she gets her back up."

"I know what I'm doing, Autumn. Try to have some faith."

"I just want the best for you," she said.

"Why do you think I haven't told you where to stick it?"

Autumn smiled as her friend headed off to bed. *Try to have some faith.* Everything in her objected to that. She trusted what she could see and sense. Faith was for fools. But for Jasmine's sake, she hoped her friend was right.

7

THE NEXT MORNING, Autumn had to rush to get ready for work. At the end of her jog, a neighbor lady, Winnie Scranton, had stopped her to promise a welcome basket and to exchange endless details about the neighborhood, the mayor and the Huffmans' weird pets.

Still nervous about work, Autumn chose her Bo-Peep white-lace bustier and fishnets for the extra confidence they provided. Wouldn't Mike's eyes pop if he saw this?

But he wasn't about to, she reminded herself. He'd be in Tucson and she'd redo the budgets while he was gone. When Lydia called, assuming Mike had asked her to, Autumn would get the scoop on the software and finally be up to the job.

She covered her stripper costume with a tailored silk dress, making it more formal with the blazer from her blue suit. She started to braid her hair, but remembered Mike's face when she'd undone it, and, instead, combed it out and left it down. She still looked professional, but she felt more relaxed.

Ready to go, she woke Jasmine, then headed out to her car. She spied the newspaper before getting in and ran it in the house for Jasmine.

Returning to her car, Autumn noticed a woman

working in the net-covered garden patch to the east of the Huffmans'.

"Hello there," Autumn said to be neighborly.

The woman squinted up at her. "You're burning my tomato leaves. You want to fix those sprinkler heads." She went back to work.

"Hmm?" Autumn stepped closer, puzzled by the woman's words.

The woman looked at her with irritation. "Here. I'll show you." She yanked off her gloves and marched to the control box on the Huffmans' wall, where she flipped a switch and a wobbly stream shot all the way to the woman's garden.

"Oh. Sorry. How do I fix that?"

"Ask Walt at the hardware store for sprinkler heads. Make him get the fresh ones from the back. And get spares. Hedgers cut off the damn things all the time."

"Thank you," she said. "I'll do that."

The woman looked at her. Under her broad hat, Autumn saw she had fierce blue eyes. Abruptly, her leathery face softened, as if with a sudden twinge of compassion. She thrust out her hand. "Barbara Dougherty," she said gruffly.

"Autumn Beshkin." She shook the hardened palm. "My friend Jasmine Ravelli and I are house-sitting for the Huffmans."

"Yeah. I hear you two driving in and out all hours of the night. Got a rough idle on that one car."

"We'll try to keep it down."

"Good. I need my sleep. So do you—" She finished with what was obviously meant as an olive branch, "If you don't want to end up wrinkled as me."

Autumn smiled. "What are you growing?" she asked.

"This and that. My specialty is peppers." She brushed back some narrow leaves to reveal a swollen red pepper. "Red fresnos. My favorite. They make the best salsa."

"And those?" Autumn pointed at some long thin ones.

"Those are arbols. They'll burn the enamel right off your teeth." She shot a quick smile at her, then stood, dusting off her hands. "Where you off dressed like that in this heat?"

"I work with the mayor—filling in for the accountant."

She gave a snort. "What we need is an auditor. The tax increase was criminal. Water service stinks. And as for trash burning—sky's black half the time. I speak out, but don't get nowhere."

Autumn had picked up a half-dozen complaints about the two percent property-tax increase from Lydia's voice mail, so she knew that was an issue. "I do know our budget is tight. Do you have specific complaints I can share with the mayor?"

The woman regarded her closely, as if to see how serious she was. "I fight my own battles." She paused, then her face softened again. "That rangy patch of lantana out back will be dead in two weeks if you don't get water to it."

"What should I do?"

"Leave 'em to die if it were me. Lantana's no better than a weed. I might have a spigot that'll help." She bent to her gardening.

Autumn wasn't sure whether or not she'd been dismissed.

"You might see the neighbors across the street," Barbara said without looking up. "The husband—

Eric—he's a halfway decent mechanic. He can fix that idle for you."

"Thanks," she said. "Have a nice day."

The woman didn't answer, just dug in with her spade.

Autumn headed into town and was surprised to see Mike's car in the parking lot. Her heart pounding, she stuck her head in his door. He was looking through some papers. "Hey," she said softly.

His eyes lit when he saw her. "Hey, yourself."

"I thought you were going to Tucson."

"In the, uh, confusion last night, I forgot the contract and the checks for the festival company. Did I leave them in your office?"

"Come and look."

He followed her into her office, which seemed smaller somehow, after the previous afternoon's make-out session. Her desk still looked awry, though they'd hurriedly put things back in place before they left.

Mike flipped through the folders in the upright rack. "Here it is. I guess it got mixed up with everything else."

"Yeah," she said, straightening the stapler.

He watched her, remembering, she'd bet, exactly how the stapler ended up on its side. "You okay?" he asked, the way new lovers questioned each other the morning after.

"I'm fine. You?" Were they standing unnaturally close? She could smell his cologne and his skin and pick out the crinkles around his dark eyes and felt a little lost in the moment.

"No bangs or shrieks, so I got some sleep."

"They're spending the night in Tucson tonight."

"So I hear." He looked at her, a million thoughts in his eyes. "Oh, Lydia says to call her. They'll be home by one."

"I feel bad bothering her."

"Newborns sleep, she says, and she'll be bored. Call her."

"Thanks, Mike. How were they? With the baby?"

"Lydia's glowing, the baby's cute except for the pointy head and Bud just laughs all the time."

"It's probably nervous relief."

"You wore your hair down," he mused.

"You said the look is casual."

"Yeah." His eyes moved restlessly over her body, taking her in, memorizing her. She wondered if he could see her costume.

"You're staring again," she said.

"I promised I'd behave, didn't I?"

"White silk bustier, pink and blue ribbons," she whispered. "Matching thong." She couldn't resist the temptation, knowing how he would react. He looked stunned.

"I didn't ask," he breathed.

"You didn't have to." She grinned.

The front door jangled. "I'm back!" Evelyn sang. "Wait'll you see what I've—" She stopped in the doorway, seeming startled. "Am I interrupting something?" She held a stack of photos.

"Nope. No. Not at all." Mike scrubbed the back of his neck.

"I've got pictures of the baby," Evelyn said, but her eyes bounced from Mike to Autumn and back, then to the floor, where Autumn noticed the wire photo holder that had been knocked from the desk. Evelyn picked it up, then placed it on the desk.

"I, um, bumped the— I knocked it over," Autumn said. She saw that her desk blotter had gotten bent over, too, and slapped it flat with a palm.

Evelyn looked at her strangely, then at Mike. "You got hives or something, Mike? Itching like that?"

"Huh?" Mike stopped rubbing his neck, his face bright red. "No. I'm fine. I'm just…anyway, let's see these pictures."

Evelyn stood between them and held up the photos.

"What a darling baby," Autumn said of the first shot, which showed a crying infant in a Day-Glo green knitted cap and gigantic matching booties. "Did you make the outfit?"

She nodded. "Did he kick up a mad fuss when I put them on. But it was worth it, don't you think?"

"Absolutely." Mike winked at Autumn over her head.

Evelyn whipped through the photos—the baby alone, with each parent, then in Evelyn's arms. Finished, she sighed. "I've got to finish that leaving-the-hospital blanket today."

"I suppose that means you won't get the business development mailing out," Mike said.

"Aren't you due in Tucson?" She gave him an accusing look.

"I'll be heading out now, yes."

"Somehow we'll carry on, won't we, Autumn?" She left, a bemused smile on her face, tapping the photos against her palm.

Mike shook his head. "Don't sit still long. She'll knit you into a cocoon."

"Do you think she suspects—"

"That I threw you onto your desk? Not in a million years."

"Really?"

"No. That wouldn't be like me at all." He shot her a grin, then rubbed his neck again.

"So did I give you hives?"

"It was a hell of a lot more fun than hives." His voice was low and sexy.

"We were as bad as Jasmine and Mark. You know they broke the covered wagon on the stage last night."

"Good Lord." He shook his head.

"Did Mike mention that he's considering moving to Phoenix?" Despite her intention not to tell him about the move, something about this exchange urged her to confide in him.

"What? No. You don't just pick up a real estate agency and set it down again. What is he thinking?"

"Same as Jasmine. That love makes all things possible."

He groaned. "Someone's going to get hurt."

"I'm afraid so." The most likely victim would be Jasmine, but Mike seemed to think Mark could get his heart broken, too.

"I'll talk to him, but I've got to get going now." He looked as though he wanted to say he would miss her. Which was so bizarre because she thought she might miss him, too. Her heart actually fluttered in her chest. *Fluttered.*

"When will you be back? So I can have the budget ready."

"I'll try to make it by five." He backed away, still watching her.

"Anything else I can do for you while you're gone?"

"Look less sexy?" He grinned. "Actually, if you can talk Dave and Rick into working out their budgets on computers instead of legal pads, I'd be eternally grateful."

"I'll try. Dave is public works and Rick is roads?"

"You got it."

"Maybe we could have dinner? If you want. Maybe early enough for the machaca burros?" Damn, she sounded far too eager.

"I'll hurry."

"Good. For the budget, I mean."

"For the budget, sure." He seemed to be trying not to get carried away, either. "If you need me, try my cell." He made the request sound intimate. They were both acting strange.

Mike left and she got to work until Evelyn popped in.

"Sorry I wasn't around much on your first day," she said, resting a hip on Autumn's desk. "I forgot to tell you the trick to the microwave. Bang it hard or it won't start. It's so old. God knows what the rays do to reproductive organs. Maybe stand back a bit—you're young. You want kids."

"I'm fine, Evelyn. Thanks."

Evelyn straightened a bent prong on the photo holder, glanced at her, then shook her head as if puzzled. "Gotta get back to my knitting. Oh, also, there are herbal teas and Swiss Miss above the sink." The phone rang and she hurried out to answer it.

The caller was Lydia and she was immensely helpful to Autumn. The best news was that the Excel spreadsheet could be imported into Lydia's system, so Autumn was relieved.

The rest of the day flew and it was nearly five when Evelyn let her know that Mike was calling for her. "Do not let the man keep you past quitting time, now," she warned.

"I'll be fine, Evelyn. Don't worry." But her heart kicked up as she pushed the blinking light. "This is Autumn."

"Hey, there," he said, his tone intimate as a lover's. "Things ran late in Tucson. How about bringing the budget to my house on a disk? We can maybe go to dinner afterward."

"No problem. Sounds nice."

"Yeah. It does." They would be alone in the house, she remembered. Mark and Jasmine were in Tucson for the night. Did he have something else in mind? Not Mike. They'd agreed, right?

Before long, she stood on the porch of a ranch-style house at the edge of town. The massive double door had a carving of a desert mountain and the doorbell echoed inside the way her heartbeat echoed in her head.

She clutched the work folder, fingers leaving sweaty marks, and held it high, turning to be sure any watching neighbor would know she was at the mayor's house on *business*.

When he opened the door and grinned, she kept her face carefully neutral. "I brought the information you needed."

He looked past her, as if to see for whom she was performing, then stepped back so she could enter a great room with high ceilings and exposed wood beams. The design was western, the layout warm and open, with white walls and chocolate accents, Navajo rugs, Indian pottery and baskets here and there, a kiva-style fireplace and brown leather furniture.

"Your home is beautiful," she said.

"Plenty of room for my brother and me."

"How was Tucson?" she asked.

"Good. Signed the contract for the carnival, put

deposits on the equipment, stands and craft booths. It's all good. Can I get you a glass of wine?"

"Sure," she said and followed him into the kitchen. He had filled a handcrafted tray with havarti, water crackers and plump purple grapes.

She popped one into her mouth. The lush fruit exploded with sweetness on her tongue. "Mmm."

He watched, smiling, then turned for the merlot, popped the cork and splashed two waiting glasses half full of wine.

"Very smooth," she said, flashing on how he'd probably perfected this activity. "This your routine for dates?"

"Hardly. I've been meeting my dates in Tucson."

"So you haven't brought anyone home to meet the neighbors? Not that it's my business."

"Not so far." He didn't seem to mind her nosiness.

"No sex, either?" She couldn't resist asking.

"That's pretty personal."

"I have no shame." She shrugged.

"Okay. Yeah, I slept with a couple of them."

"And?" No shame at all.

"It was fine."

"Not fiery. Not intense?"

He looked at her. "It was fine," he repeated, as if protecting the women's reputations.

"Just meaningless sex, then." She couldn't leave the man alone. She enjoyed the surprise of his answers—sometimes serious, sometimes wry, sometimes vulnerable.

"Sex is never meaningless. Sometimes it means more than other times."

"How is that?"

"Depending on the people and how they feel about each other." He ticked his wineglass against hers. "Don't you agree?"

"I guess. Sure." What would sex between them mean? She watched his fingers slide around the big belly of his glass the way it might on her skin. He'd gone lighter on the cologne today and she picked up the smell of outdoors and the leather of his car. "How did you meet your dates?"

"How did I meet them? Hmm." He set his glass down and leaned on his forearms. "You have to promise not to laugh."

"Cross my heart." She made an *X* over her chest.

He leveled a look at her. "Right. Just don't laugh hard. I subscribe to a dating service for professionals."

"Really?" She thought only losers and married cheaters used dating services. "I guess that makes sense," she said slowly. "If you're too busy to troll the bars and you're serious about finding Mrs. Mayor."

"I am serious."

"But isn't it kind of weird with a service? Checklists and preferences and 'I love sunset swims and calico cats' crap? What about chemistry?"

"That's most important to you? Chemistry?"

"I'm not looking for anyone steady, remember?"

"For you it's just the sex, then?" His eyes held hers, bored in, wanting more. That confessor/therapist thing again.

"Yep." There was chemistry here, for sure, sizzling all over the place.

"And that works?"

"If you're clear about it."

"And you're always clear?"

"Crystal."

"I see." He pondered that.

She plopped a triangle of cheese onto a cracker, but her hand shook so hard the cheese fell right off.

He caught it and extended it to her mouth. When her tongue touched his finger he began to shake, too. They were all alone in this beautiful house with a kitchen countertop plenty big enough to hold them both.

She had to change the subject fast. "So should we get to work?"

"First a toast." He tapped his glass against hers. His dark eyes looked good against the deep purple wine he held out. "To us. To me getting a life, and to you—?"

"Building my future." She tapped his glass.

"Yeah." He paused. "Waitress to an accountant. You should be proud."

"I have a long way to go."

"Still. It must have taken years to save the money."

Strippers made a hell of a lot more money than waitresses, but she wasn't about to point that out. "So, about you getting a life," she said to change the subject, "I think you should do that bowling team thing Celia mentioned."

"Are you kidding?" He laughed, then looked at her. "Would you be on my team?"

"I'm not very good."

"So, I'll teach you. I taught you to golf, remember?"

"Then, okay. Why not?" It might be fun.

"You, me and Evelyn—I know she'll play—that's three. We need two more—Dave and Rick or Page. Evelyn will be thrilled."

"Good. Celia will think I'm a good influence on you."

"Your influence on me isn't all good," he said,

smiling. "Let's get to work in my office." They carried their wine into a den area off the living room and looked over what she'd done. Mike was pleased and made only minor changes on the report.

They were focused, working steadily, when Autumn heard a sound from deeper in the house. Someone panting? Then a moan, a groan and a shriek. It was as if oversexed ghosts were haunting the place.

"Sounds like they got back from Tucson early," Mike said.

An "Ohhh" swelled, like a train building steam.

"No kidding."

"Mark's car was in the garage, so I assumed they took hers."

The moans built, became rhythmic and Autumn pushed to her feet, extremely uncomfortable.

"I'll put on some music." Mike went to the stereo, but fumbled the CD, which fell and rolled across the rug to Autumn's feet.

She carried it to him. "Maybe I should leave."

"You shouldn't have to go just because—". He stopped as the moan train down the hall built up to a head, and met Autumn's gaze. He was so close she felt his body heat. She licked her lips and he licked his own. "Why does this keep happening?" he asked.

"It's the company we keep."

"It's more than that. If you didn't work for me, Autumn…"

"What?"

"You know exactly what," he said, low, his voice a growl.

"I think I do." There was sex going on down the hall and, dammit, she wanted some, too. She was starving for it. This time, she took charge. She grabbed Mike's shirt, yanked him close and kissed him hard.

He kissed her back, tasting of warm merlot and sweet breath and she wanted to just stand here and keep kissing until she melted clean away.

Except now they could hear big bare feet slapping tile and heading their way. They broke their embrace, but the footsteps veered off—toward the kitchen?

"I'll see what's going on," Mike said. "Stay here."

Still caught in the heat of the moment, she could only nod. She'd been making out with her boss, for God's sake.

And all she wanted was to keep on doing it.

8

MIKE FOUND HIS BROTHER beside the open refrigerator, stark naked and holding a can of whipping cream.

"Damn!" Mark grabbed a dish towel and held it to his waist, letting the refrigerator door bang shut. "What the hell are you doing here?"

"I live here. You're supposed to be in Tucson."

He was startled to realize he was pissed that Mark's presence kept him from taking Autumn to bed—a distinctly short-sighted thought. Not like him at all.

"We finished early and couldn't check in, so we just came home." He shrugged, acting not at all embarrassed to be standing with a plaid cloth pressed to his crotch.

"And now dessert?" Mike nodded at the whipped cream.

"Exactly." Mark shook the can, then squirted some into his mouth, tilting it toward Mike. "Want some?"

He shook his head. "Autumn's here, by the way. We're, uh, working."

"We'll keep it down." Mark didn't doubt him for an instant. Was Mike really that work-obsessed?

"What's this I hear about you moving to Phoenix?" he said, more crankily than he'd intended.

Mark grimaced. "I was going to tell you when I had it all worked out."

"You have commitments here, Mark, not to mention a business, too—"

"I *know*. I'll wrap everything up, find a replacement for the Chamber and the econ committee. I'm not leaving next week, Mike. Relax."

"It takes years to build a real estate business in a new city."

"I know that, too. I'll contact some brokers in Phoenix and do some networking. It's a big city and real estate is booming."

Mike stared at his brother. "I hate to remind you what happened last time."

"You think this is like with Brenda? It's not. You know, your über brother routine is starting to get old. What makes you think I don't know my own heart?"

"Past history," he snapped, instantly sorry he'd said it.

Mark shook his head. "I'm going to give you the benefit of the doubt and assume you're just trying to look out for me, as misguided as that is." He was clearly angry.

"I am. I'm just—"

"Being you, yeah. Here's what I wish. I wish you'd get your own life—hell, your own problems—so you'd run out of time to mess with mine." A muscle ticked in his cheek.

Mike had gone too far, he knew, but he didn't want to see Mark wrecked again.

"Hey…" They turned to find Jasmine standing there wearing one of Mark's shirts. "I heard voices."

At the sight of her, all the fight went out of Mark. "Just my brother," he said softly. "Autumn's out in the living room."

"Really?" She widened her eyes. "What's she doing here?"

"Working," Mark said.

Mike's face flamed.

"Okay…" Jasmine grinned. At least *one* person believed him capable of something wild.

"Oh, he's serious," Mark said. "My big brother is all about the work. Have you turned her into a workaholic, too?"

"Oh, she's into that already," Jasmine said. "Is she doing okay on the job?"

"She's doing great. She learns fast." *And kisses great.* And every time he thought of her the earth shifted under his feet.

"She doesn't believe how smart she is," Jasmine said, "so she gets all testy and worries about me instead."

"That sounds familiar," Mark said, shooting him a look before pulling Jasmine close to him.

She smiled up at him with such contentment that Mike felt like an intruder.

He felt something else—*envious*. He wanted what they had. He wanted to put his arm around the woman he loved and have her look up at him with trust and desire. He wanted to feel that heat, that bond, that closeness.

Maybe he was acting wild with Autumn out of envy for Mark. Which was ridiculous. Mark was having an affair with a stripper. Talk about worlds colliding. What had Autumn said? *Love makes all things possible.*

Only in the movies. You didn't fall in love overnight and run away from your life. Mark had his business and his future to consider. Hell, his reputation.

Mike could see how someone as flamboyant and exciting as Jasmine could sweep a guy off his feet. Mike was no prude. It was Jasmine's business if she wanted to get naked for strangers, though he didn't see

Mark putting up with that for long. Mark was a one-woman man and pretty old-fashioned about love.

"Are we having a party?" Autumn stepped into the kitchen, her folder under one arm, purse over the other. She put her wineglass on the counter. She was flushed and glanced at him, then away, as if afraid to make eye contact.

"We could," Jasmine said, taking a sip of Autumn's wine. "Mmm. Pour me some of this."

Mark clutched the towel. "I'll go put on some clothes."

"No need," Autumn said. "I have to get back to the house and take care of the pets."

"We weren't finished with that project." Mike sounded so tense he couldn't believe Mark and Jasmine didn't catch on.

"We're done," Autumn said. "I left you a printout. If you want any more changes, call me before I make copies in the morning. Your meeting's at nine?"

He wanted time to at least talk about what had happened. "Let me take you to dinner." He couldn't catch her gaze.

"I'm not hungry." She smiled faintly.

"God, let him buy you supper," Mark said. "The man works you to death on saltines and Velveeta?" He indicated the plate of expensive cheese and crackers Mike had carefully prepared.

"Thanks anyway," she said and headed for the door.

Mike followed. "Listen, Autumn, I—"

She raised her hand. "That was crazy, Mike. This is better. I'll see you in the morning." She turned and hurried toward her car.

He started to call her back, but she had a point.

They'd been acting like Mark and Jasmine. In a way it was his fault. A childish envy of his brother's affair and the desire to escape from his life had combined to make him behave like a lust-crazed lunatic. He was Autumn's boss, for God's sake.

He felt trapped, in a way, by who he was and what he stood for. Trapped by duty, by style, by life.

Mark thought Mike preferred being in charge. Not exactly true. He'd love to hand off for a while, do what *he* wanted for a change. One day, he'd talk someone into running for mayor and kick back and take stock of his life.

He'd worked too hard for too long, which was probably why a mysterious beauty could knock him to the ground with one kiss. Not to mention her underwear.

That settled, he got in his car to hit the diner for supper, but he couldn't stop thinking about Autumn. She stayed in his head, made him want to play hooky from his life, bury himself in her body, never get out of bed or come up for air.

What was it about the woman? She was smart and funny and edgy. She woke him up from a life-long doze. She made him want to let go of the rope and just drop into the moment, the wild rush of what might happen between them.

He wanted to help her, too. There was a grittiness about her that said she'd seen too much of human nature and it had hurt her. She needed someone to give her hope, show her the bright side. Someone like him?

Stop it. He ground his palms on the steering wheel so that the leather squeaked. Frustration rose in a sweaty wave, never mind the AC chasing the remains of the day's heat from his car.

He needed to hit something hard. Like golf balls?

What a good idea that had been—even in the dark. The six they'd whacked were still out on the fairway.

Before he headed into the diner, he stepped into Walt's hardware store and grabbed two boxes of cheap balls. If he didn't feel better after supper and a Tecate, he'd have twenty-four chances to slam out his frustration. The way he felt right now, those balls would end up halfway to Tucson.

AUTUMN COULD HARDLY see to drive when she left Mike's house. She yearned for Mike. *Yearned.* An emotion from the days when it was honorable to repress human needs and natural urges.

Standing in the kitchen with the half-dressed couple, she'd wanted to drag Mike to the nearest bed and go at it, no questions asked, no doubts allowed.

She didn't feel much better now. What was she going to do with this agonizing hunger, this itchy craving for the man? She was almost crazy with frustration.

Pulling into the garage, she noticed a set of golf clubs against the back wall next to a wire basket of dirt-daubed balls. The Huffmans evidently golfed. Perfect.

She fed the pets and herself, changed into shorts and a tank top, threw a club and the bucket of balls into the trunk and set off for Desert Paradise. Slamming those balls into the sky would have to help.

When she turned into the parking lot, though, she saw Mike's Saab already there. She made him out standing at the first tee and she felt a jolt, as though her heart had been hit with electric paddles.

He started toward her and she went to open the trunk.

"Frustrated?" he asked with a wry grin, taking the bucket of balls from her fingers.

"You, too?"

He showed her his palm, streaked with red where blisters would form.

"Poor baby." She cupped his hand. "Should have worn gloves."

He only looked at her, his dark eyes flaring with heat.

What did it mean that they'd met out here again? Would they hit a few balls and go home? Or would something else happen?

"Let's set up a row of balls," he said, taking back his hand, "and talk."

They spaced the balls a foot apart, gleaming in the moonlight like eggs in an Easter hunt. From opposite ends of the row they took practice swings.

"Ready?" he called to her.

"Ready," she called back.

He whacked his first ball high and hard.

"Nice shot," she said, but he wasn't even looking at where the ball had gone. He was staring at her. "What should we do about this?" he asked.

"I don't know." She swung and hit her first ball, medium power, low as a line drive. "Maybe go for it?"

"Maybe," he said. Whack. He hit his ball high and hard. They watched it disappear, then looked at each other. She could see he was breathing as hard as she was.

"Why shouldn't we?" she said, swinging and missing.

"Because we work together," he said grimly.

"Right. Sex at work is a bad idea." They both swung hard and the balls went high and straight out.

"Worse, I'm your boss." Whack. Mike's ball went so fast she could hardly follow its path.

"This internship means everything to me." She swung so fiercely the club's vibration hurt her hand.

Mike whistled at the arc of her ball, then looked at her. "How can I tell my brother not to think with his equipment when that's what I'd be doing?" He steadied his swing before hitting the ball so violently it sounded as though it had split in two.

"Same with Jasmine." Whack. That one stung so she shook out her hand.

"You okay?" Mike asked softly. Only four balls separated them now. "What if we didn't tell them?" He didn't bother to swing.

"It's a small town. You can't keep secrets."

"True." He paused, thinking, then hit a ball so softly she saw where it stopped. When he lifted his gaze to her, his eyes were shining with longing.

"We could be discreet," she said, stepping over a ball.

"Not let this interfere with work." He stepped over another.

"You do need to get a life," she said, kicking a ball out of the way. "It could be just while I'm here. A summer thing."

"You make me want that, Autumn." He kicked away the last ball so they stood toe to toe. He took a ragged breath.

"You make me want you," she said, the words aching in her throat, her body trembling to be against his. She tossed her club to the left. He tossed his to the right and they threw their arms around each other.

The kiss was eager and desperate at first. Then they

took turns panicking. First, Autumn broke it off, but Mike brought her back with more fervent kisses. Then Mike retreated, so she held him tighter and kissed him deeper until he met her with equal intensity.

They kept up the intimate struggle for long minutes while the wind whistled through the feathery mesquites and cicadas kicked up a hum that seemed to buzz in Autumn's bloodstream.

Finally, Mike broke off. "There's a blanket in my car."

"Let's get it," she said, swaying, feeling weak.

"It'll be dusty."

"Who cares?" She kissed him again.

He pulled back, fighting to speak. "What about protection?"

"I'm on the pill. Are you healthy?"

"Yeah."

"Perfect. Let's go." She kissed him again, relieved they'd decided. She shut away all doubts and worries, took his hand and ran to his car for the blanket then deep onto the course to a stand of mesquite, where they spread the blanket in the softness of last season's leaves.

They took off their shirts and she was so glad she'd gone without a bra. Mike grasped her breasts and she leaned into his hand, loving his strong fingers on her, the sensation of air on her bare upper body.

"You are so beautiful."

She ran her palms across his chest. His skin shivered beneath her fingers and he grasped her wrists, looked at her, letting his heat and hunger tell her they weren't playing around anymore.

They stripped the rest of the way and Autumn fell

back onto the blanket. Mike rose over her, sucking one nipple deeply into his mouth, his erection brushing her belly.

She bent her legs, open to him. "Inside me. I want you there." She craved his body, wanted them joined as one. The need beat inside her like a drum, relentless and primitive and overpowering. She'd never felt so carnal, so needy, before.

Mike eased into her, deep, and held himself there, looking down at her, backlit by silver moonlight. "I'm here."

"You feel good." She was relieved to be filled up by him and even more aroused. She lifted her hips and he bent to kiss her before he thrust in and out, deep, then deeper.

They moved in an easy rhythm, their bodies moving as one, with equal need, equal speed and force. There was something dangerous about how easy this was, but Autumn focused on the pleasure that grew with each pump of his cock, each lift of her hips.

She cried out, her voice carrying on the quiet breeze.

Mike thrust in and out, again and again. She dug her fingers into his back, her clitoris swelled, tightened to readiness. "I'm close," she said and her climax flared like the time-lapse blossoming of a flower, silent and stunning in its beauty and surprise.

Mike stilled, then exploded into her. She felt it deep in her body.

They rode the feeling, holding each other, and Autumn felt herself disappear into the moment, surprised to feel so safe. When she came to herself, Mike's arms were tight around her. She breathed in his cologne, his clean sweat and the smells of the desert.

She let it all wash through her. She didn't try to muscle the moment into a shape she liked. She didn't fight it or try to define it. She just let it be.

She felt so happy under the stars lying on Mike's chest, listening to his heart gradually slow.

"I can't believe we're naked on a golf course." His voice was husky with emotion.

"I love sex outdoors," she breathed.

"It's a first for me." He kissed the top of her head, stroked her hair.

"You've lived a sheltered life, Mike Fields."

"Oh, yeah?" He shifted to look down at her, an eyebrow lifted, looking so sexy her heart turned over in her chest.

"You're escaping from your life, right? Sex is the best escape. So many positions, so many places. And a long, hot month ahead of us."

"Sounds pretty good. Not like me at all, but something I want to try." He chuckled, his breathing easy. "I haven't felt this relaxed in…I don't know…."

"Ever? Have you ever felt this relaxed, Mr. Responsible?" she teased, rising on her elbow so they were face-to-face on their sides.

"You have a point.

"Were you always like this?"

"Since our parents died, I think. It was a car wreck when I was sixteen. Mark was thirteen and Heidi was six."

"Heidi told me the story. So terrible. You moved in with relatives, right?"

"Our aunt and uncle, yeah, but they were older and hadn't had kids. They did a lot of hovering and hand-wringing because they felt sorry for us. It just didn't work well."

"What do you mean?"

"Heidi and Mark were very quiet so my aunt and uncle tried buying things—every video game Mark mentioned, every Barbie or outfit that caught Heidi's fancy. They let Mark play 24/7, even fake sick days to stay home. He convinced them Gatorade was a good breakfast. Heidi spent school nights with friends until she was cranky and completely exhausted."

"But your aunt and uncle were doing their best, right?"

"Of course. They just didn't know how to be parents. So I stepped in."

Autumn's mother had done her best, too, despite her personal grudges and constant crises and terrible temper. Autumn had long ago forgiven her. Better never to expect too much. "What did you do?"

"I set up a schedule, made rules, assigned chores. The kids sulked and I helped my aunt and uncle get through that."

"That's a lot of responsibility for a sixteen-year-old."

"It was good for me. I was too busy refereeing whose turn it was for dishes to feel sorry for myself. It felt natural to take charge. It's who I am, I guess."

"What about your social life? Did you have time for friends? A girl?"

"I didn't have a real girlfriend until college." He gave a wistful smile.

"Tell me about her," she said, running her fingers down his chest, loving the feel of his skin. She felt no urge to leave. Maybe because they weren't trapped in a room, but free under the stars. Or maybe because she felt so comfortable with Mike. He seemed familiar as an old friend.

"That was a long time ago." He brushed her hair

away from her face, touched her cheek, looking at her with so much emotion, she hoped the moonlight was playing tricks on her eyes.

"Tell me," she said again.

"Her name was Moira and she was smart and funny and ambitious. A journalism major. She wanted to be a foreign correspondent." He stroked her arm gently, his fingers soft and sure, as though they knew her body by heart. "She got a fellowship with an international journalism group. She wanted me to come with her, but I couldn't. Heidi was in middle school and it was Mark's turn for college soon and the family business needed me."

"So you gave up the woman you loved to do the big brother thing?" It seemed sad to her.

He shrugged. "We were so young. We would have gone our separate ways soon enough. This town is my home. Yeah, sometimes I want to escape, but who doesn't? Haven't you ever wanted to run away from your life?"

"I did run away. Dropped out of high school when I was sixteen. Worked in restaurants until I was old enough to serve drinks, then did cocktail waitressing." *And when my little brother needed fast cash, I became a stripper.* Keeping her brother out of jail didn't sound like such a noble sacrifice. She and Mike were from different worlds entirely. He was a friend, but only up to a point.

"And now you're back in school. Which is great."

"I just hope I can stick it out."

"Of course you will."

She closed her eyes and flopped back onto the blanket. "It's not that easy. I tend to quit when things get tough."

"I don't believe that. You sure were determined to get this job."

"That was different."

"What have you quit anyway?"

"It all started with the school play." She laughed, knowing how silly the incident would sound—at the time she'd been wrecked by it.

"What happened?"

"I was goofing around mimicking a rock star outside algebra class and my teacher convinced me I should audition for the school musical—*West Side Story*. She played piano for the drama coach. So, for the hell of it, I auditioned."

"And you got the part?"

"Yeah. Anita. I couldn't believe it." She'd been so happy she slipped and told her mother without figuring out how best to present the news.

"My mom hassled me. Said I was pretending to be better than I was." *Play dress up if you want, but trash is trash to them, and they'll treat you that way.*

"Why would she do that?"

"She didn't want me to get hurt. I figured out later also that she counted on my money from the diner where I worked nights and weekends, but she was too proud to say that."

"Not very loving of her."

"She did the best she could with what she had to give. I tried to forget what she'd said, but it stuck in my head. I figured that my algebra teacher begged the drama coach to take me and they both felt sorry for me. The drama kids all knew each other, so they ignored me. I got nervous and goofed up a lot, blew my cues. It felt like everyone was wondering what the hell I was doing there, so I quit."

"That's a shame," he said.

"I know. I should have stuck it out."

"It's understandable, Autumn. Everyone's insecure in high school. And your mother should have been your biggest fan."

"Don't blame her. She did her best. She was limited, that's all. Besides, lots of kids with bad parents go to college, get good jobs, raise families, pay taxes. Look at you—you lost your parents at sixteen and you're the damn town father."

"Who says that means I came out fine?"

"You came out better than me. I have a habit of quitting. I like the easy road. There was a work-study program I crapped out on, it took forever to get my GED…other things." She'd missed a semester at ASU, too, when she saw how much work it would be.

"Starting over is scary. People get into a rut and just stay where they are. Like me. I'm kind of stuck."

She looked at him. He had such a clear sense of his place in the world it surprised her that he had doubts.

"I don't know how you used to be," he said, "but you're sure going for what you want now. Maybe you've changed or maybe you never gave yourself enough credit."

"I don't know." She felt an odd confusion, as if she'd been seeing the world wrong. She'd never talked about her views on her life with a man before. Maybe she had trapped herself. What would Mike say if he knew about her other career? She didn't want to know.

"You know, it's not too late for you, Mike. Hell, take flying lessons. Start a flight school."

He chuckled. "You know, lying here like this with you, anything seems possible."

"I know," she breathed, surprised by how open her heart felt, as wide and limitless as the desert sky above.

"You make me want more." Something in his voice scared her. They couldn't want more. They had plenty right here and she had to remind them both.

"You make me want this." She ran her hands down his chest, across his stomach to where he was already hard for her again.

"Mmm. Good idea."

She rose to her knees and he slid in deep and easy.

"This is so good," he said, looking up at her in wonder.

"It is. So good." And she vowed to relish every moment. They didn't need more than what they'd agreed to—a vacation for him, a confidence boost for her. That was all it could be.

9

WHAT UNDERWEAR DID she have on?

Mike risked a glance down the table at Autumn during the council meeting. So far today, with the rush of preparing for the meeting, they'd only had time to exchange guilty grins.

"What do you think, Mike?" Rick asked.

"Excuse me?" Mike drew his attention to the roads manager, who'd asked something about the budgets. He fought to focus through the thick fog that lingered from his night with Autumn. *Stop acting like Mark, dammit.*

He was handling the situation much better than his brother. He and Autumn had set sensible limits. They would be discreet, stick to work during work hours, but spend every other possible second naked in each other's arms. Very sensible.

"Could you run that by me again?" he asked. "I was distracted." He caught Autumn's quick grin and felt his face flame. He hoped he wasn't giving himself away before they'd even started the affair.

No one gave him any strange looks, though, and when the meeting was over he had to steady himself not to follow Autumn into her office and back her against the door or clear her desk to go for it all the way.

Too crazy. But he did need to touch base with her about the logistics for tonight. Except she was still in the conference room talking to Dave and Rick.

"I could see that you sweated blood over your numbers," Autumn was saying to the men, who stood close to her, grinning like idiots. How could they resist her? No one could. "I can show you how to make the numbers come out easy-breezy."

"Oh, yeah?" Dave said, clearly under her spell.

"Really?" Rick said, smitten, too.

"Cross my heart." Autumn crossed her lapels, flirting just enough to draw them in. "It's even got an automatic calculator. Wouldn't it be nice to not have to do all that math? Just—poof—the totals show up?"

"Tell us more." Rick said.

"Yeah," Dave added. Those two old coots were eating it up. Mike watched as she charmed them into her office to show them how a spreadsheet acted like a calculator. Just like that she'd cajoled them into taking the plunge into modern office procedures.

She'd gotten him to hire her the same way. She'd charmed him, too. *Pushed it* was how she put it. It made him seem manipulable, but what the hell. They had a connection now. It was just a summer thing—a vacation—but he felt something more bubbling under the surface.

He took care of some festival business, talked to another small-town mayor about some business leads, all the while half-listening for Dave and Rick to leave Autumn's office.

When he heard her in the kitchen, he ended his call quickly and headed in, mug in hand as an excuse, and found her making tea.

He slopped coffee into his mug. "So…Dave and Rick—"

"I miss you," she said, cutting him off, looking eager and nervous.

"I miss you, too," he whispered, glad he wasn't alone in the feeling. He sipped his coffee absently, completely unable to take his eyes from her face. "I want to be inside—"

"Hey, save some for me!" Evelyn headed toward them.

"—the final stretch," he finished in a louder voice, stepping away from Autumn. "Coming up on the end of the race, right?" Huh? A dumb sports analogy was better than declaring he wanted to be inside Autumn in front of Evelyn, who was pouring coffee into her mug, oblivious to the vibe.

"So what do you think about 'Town Hall Terrors' as a name?" she said. Dave and Rick had agreed to be on their bowling team.

"Sounds wicked," Autumn said. "I like being wicked, don't you, Mayor Mike." She looked right at him.

"Uh, sure," he said, not as good at faking it as she was.

"I'm thinking I'll make a bowling ball with horns and a devil tail for the shirt decal," Evelyn mused, stirring creamer into her coffee. "League night's tomorrow, so tonight we practice."

"Tonight?" Mike said. He wanted to be with Autumn tonight. And every night all month long.

"The tournament's in three weeks. Come on. We've got to work out the kinks." She sipped her coffee. "Ew. This is ice cold. How can you drink that?" She nodded at the mug he'd been drinking from. He hadn't tasted a drop.

"That pot's going south. It doesn't stay hot for five minutes. I'll get a new one with petty cash. Oh, and I'll pick up the shirts, too. Large for the men, medium for the women, extra large for Dave's beer gut?" She poured her coffee out in the sink. "Be back fast."

"Take your time," Mike said, still watching Autumn.

When Evelyn was gone, Autumn said, "Now what was that you were saying about being inside something?"

"You. I want to be inside you."

She shivered. "I know. But now we're bowling."

"Yeah. Now that I have you, I don't need a hobby."

"You can come over after," she offered, eyes lit with hope.

"It'll be late. What'll the neighbors think?"

"Hmm. Good point. We have to be sneaky. I've got it—I'll pick you up in my car. You hide until I get in the garage."

"Sounds crazy. Maybe we should forget it tonight."

"I'm wearing the black bra with the open nipples again."

Heat washed through him in a wave. "Ouch. Okay. I'm in." He couldn't believe he was even considering such cloak-and-dagger stunts, but he was. "What made you buy that bra, anyway?"

She went strangely pale. The question had hit her wrong, he realized. "Oh. I, um, just wanted to feel sexy."

"Well, it worked," he said, relieved when she smiled. He realized there was a lot about Autumn he didn't know. He only hoped a month would be enough time to find it all out.

ALL AFTERNOON, WHILE SHE SENT out the water, sewage and garbage bills and started on the tax assessments, Mike's question snagged Autumn's thoughts like a rough cuticle on silk. Why had she bought the sexy bra? *To strip out of it in front of hungry-eyed men. To turn them on, make them want me.*

But why dwell on that? Or even tell Mike? The plan was to give Mike a vacation and have some fun herself. There was no point in telling him about her other career. He might not react well. She wanted to see lust and longing in his dark eyes, not shock and judgment.

Toward the end of the day, she searched for grants on the Arizona Cities and Towns Web site. Maybe she was sleeping with her boss, but she would be an exceptional intern all the same. She found two great ones—a rural health care grant for childhood vaccinations and a federal historic preservation grant that would work for the old Copper Corners buildings.

The search made her run late with the license expiration reminders, so she told Mike she'd meet him at the bowling alley.

After a quick shower, she reached the team's lane just as everyone was trying on Evelyn's shirts.

Mike caught her gaze, heat and delight in his eyes, but he greeted her in a big, jokey voice, "Ready to kick ass and take names, Beshkin?"

"I'm afraid I'm your weakest link."

"We'll help you, won't we?" He directed the question at the team, but took her to the farthest table so she could put on her shoes. They were almost private, which made it perfect.

"Can you get that for me?" she asked innocently,

pointing to where one of her shoes had fallen. She angled her body in Mike's line of sight and when he bent, she separated her legs for him, her heart racing. She was revealing herself to a man she *wanted* and it felt new and scary, like walking off a cliff hoping there would be a net.

Mike noticed and froze. He lifted his eyes to hers, his gaze hot. "You're not wearing any—"

She pressed her fingers to her mouth in pretend surprise. "Well, shoot. I knew I forgot something."

He glanced around to be certain no one was nearby and when it appeared safe, checked her out again.

Her heart pounded so hard she thought it might explode, but she forced herself to sound cool. "Is that a bowling pin in your pants or are you just glad to see me?"

"You expect me to bowl like this?" he growled.

"You needed a handicap, Mayor Mike." She finished tying her shoes.

His eyes glittered at her. "Just wait until I get you alone."

"I can't wait." The idea made her shiver.

He groaned. "I'll never make it through a whole game."

"So do you know anything about balls, Mayor Mike?" she asked, standing shakily. She was as dazed as he was.

"Besides the fact that mine are blue?" he muttered, taking her elbow. "Come on, you." He led her to the racks and helped her choose a lightweight green ball. They took their time, letting their fingers brush, and she hoped they weren't being too obvious. It was delicious and tantalizing and Autumn ached for him.

Mike demonstrated how to throw the ball and she tried to use his tips—back straight, shoulders square, concentrate—which wasn't easy with him so close. But somehow her third ball managed to slam into the triangle of pins for a strike.

"Looks like we've been hustled," Mike said to the rest of the team, who all congratulated her.

At the vent, where she dried her sweaty fingers, she leaned close to Mike. "I play better when I'm wet."

A shudder passed through him and she loved it. She was aware that he was trying not to stare at her denim skirt, which flirted with her bare bottom. She knew she was covered—strippers know exactly what shows and when—but Mike didn't and she liked that he was nervous.

"Keep that pin in your pants for me," she whispered and nodded toward the restrooms. She sashayed off, deliberately letting her hips swing, knowing Mike couldn't help staring at her. It was great to have a sensible, responsible guy practically losing control because of how sexy she was.

The two-stall ladies' room was in the middle of being redecorated. It smelled of new paint, pictures were braced on the floor, the tile grout looked damp and the door was freshly sanded and covered in fine yellow dust.

She was washing her hands at the sink when the door opened and she looked into the mirror and saw Mike. She spun into his arms and grabbed his backside with her dripping-wet hands. "What are you doing?"

"What you want me to do," he said, backing into the door, pulling her to him, kissing her hard.

She turned the lock beside his hip so no one could come in.

Mike lifted her body, turning to brace her against

the freshly tiled wall and she wrapped her legs around his waist.

Her skirt was short and she wore no panties, so it was mere seconds before Mike was inside her.

"What else could I do when you spread your legs for me out there? So wet and ready."

"I was. I am." The rush was so intense she feared she might pass out. Mike was so hot for her he'd attacked her in the women's room. "This is crazy," she breathed.

"But you love it." He pumped into her hard.

"I do. I love it. Hard. Go hard." Each stroke drove her closer to release. She was completely swept away by this man in this moment, knowing only that she wanted him deep inside her.

"You make me forget everything but you," he said, thrusting into her. "You're all I want. I see you and I have to have you." He was as lost as she was.

She gasped for air, forgot to exhale. She wished they were naked, body to body, but it was enough that he filled her, eased the burn, the ache, the hunger and it was so good. *Goodgoodgood.*

"I'm coming," she whispered and buried her face in the denim of his shirt so her cry wouldn't make someone call 911.

Mike said her name and came, shuddering with the power of it. He kissed her hair, her cheek, her forehead, her nose, panting for air, still holding her tight.

She allowed her legs to drop to the floor.

"Are you okay? Did I hurt you?"

"No. That was…amazing." She'd had take-me-now sex before, but it had never been this intense, as vital as life.

He chuckled into her hair, ran his hands down her arms. "You make me crazy, you know that?"

"All part of getting a life."

"Yeah. A life." They were still standing in a daze when they heard steps approach.

"Shit." Mike started for a stall, but the intruder didn't try the door. Instead, they heard rapid chatter— a girl, probably on a cell phone.

"How am I going to get out of here?" he said.

"I'll distract her." She straightened her skirt and left the lavatory to stand in front of the teenage girl talking on the phone, her back to the restrooms. "Excuse me," she said, "but can you tell me where the high school is?"

The girl looked at Autumn as if she had to be brain dead not to know. "Just down Main. The building with big columns?"

"Thanks so much. I'm new in town." Over the girl's shoulder, she saw Mike emerge, then angle himself as if he'd just left the men's room.

They'd pulled it off, she thought, then noticed two distinct sawdust handprints on his ass. She'd grabbed him with wet hands right before he leaned against the sanded door.

She rushed to catch up and brush away the marks.

"What are you doing?" He looked around, but she'd already made certain no one was watching.

"Removing the evidence." She gave his butt a squeeze.

"Keep it up and I'll snap in two. Then where will you be?"

"Miserable," she said. She let him walk back to the team alone, hoping no one would put two and two together.

By the time practice was over, Autumn was burning for Mike again. She followed him to his house in her car at a discreet distance, where he parked, then sneaked into her backseat like a spy.

Small towns. It seemed ridiculous to her, but the illicit thrill of hiding their affair added to the excitement.

"I can't wait to touch you." Mike's voice from behind her seat made her shiver. "In fact…I won't wait." Then he reached between the seats and his fingers found her under her skirt.

"Oh, don't…I can't…" Her entire body shook with the electric rush of it. She almost drove off the road.

"I want you to come for me." He stroked her, slow and steady. He was not about to stop, so she pulled over, slammed on the brakes, and leaned her head back while he finished her off, her thighs tight, body rocking with an orgasm so explosive that she shrieked, the sound loud in the closed car.

"Now drive," Mike ordered. "I want you naked."

She sagged forward, beeping the horn, which made her yelp, then laugh. Mike's deep voice joined her in a low chuckle.

She shakily drove home and pulled into the garage.

Inside, the cats circled their legs, meowing. "I've got to feed these guys. Have a seat." She motioned at the family room sofa and Mike went to sit.

While she prepared the mix of wet and dry food, she was surprised to see the cats crowd around Mike, instead of lurking near their dishes. Marmalade curled onto his lap and Mocha planted himself behind Mike's head on the sofa.

"Looks like you've made friends," she said.

He petted Marmalade. "Nice cats. You about done?"

"Let me just take out the trash."

"*Then* can we go to bed?" He sounded as impatient as a kid waiting for birthday gifts.

"Yes," she breathed.

"Hurry up. I want to taste you."

She shuddered. She'd been lusted after before, but this seemed different—bigger somehow. She felt essential to him. It would worry her except that she knew they'd set solid limits.

When she opened the kitchen door, she was surprised to find a box at her feet. It held a sprinkler, a plastic bag of red chiles, a crockery bowl of what looked like salsa wrapped in cellophane with a recipe card on top. Had to be from Barbara Dougherty, her cranky neighbor.

She glanced over at the woman's house and noticed a shape against the curtain in a lighted window. As she watched, the light went out. The woman had been watching for Autumn to get her gift. She found herself smiling as she carried the box into the house.

The first sex was fast and frantic and wordless in the creaky guest bed where Autumn slept, fueled by need and the hours at the bowling alley. Usually, she liked more of a performance, but the raw act was all she needed with Mike.

After that, Mike went down on her. He seemed honestly happy to have his mouth on her, licking and sucking with such apparent pleasure that she just lay back and enjoyed. Lots of men went through the motions with oral sex, but not Mike. He took his time, knew what he was doing and sent rush after rush of pleasure through her body.

When she came, she felt the sting of tears. So strange. Somehow, being with Mike felt solid, real, right.

She took him into her mouth next, loving every moment, joyfully swallowing his release. They kept going—missionary style first, then rolling over so she was on top and ending on their sides, face-to-face, seeing the power of their mutual climax in each other's eyes.

Finally, they collapsed, panting, weak and sweaty, onto the narrow mattress. Autumn had never felt more content.

The two cats, whom she usually only saw at dinnertime, jumped onto the bed and curled at their feet, suddenly content, too. It had to be Mike. Mike made everyone feel at home.

After a bit, hunger sent her to the kitchen, where she assembled a tray of her neighbor's salsa, chips and beers.

Mike was suitably appreciative. He crunched a salsa-loaded chip. "The salsa's great. You make it?"

"No. My neighbor, Barbara Dougherty, gave it to me."

Mike stopped, mid-chew. "Barbara Dougherty gave you food? How did that happen?"

She shrugged. "I don't know. I talked to her about her garden, I guess."

"You did something, all right. The woman has a complaint at every public meeting. Too much trash burning, the water and sewer bills are wrong, taxes are too high, on and on."

"Yeah. She complained about the tax increase. I explained the budget was tight."

"And she bought that?"

"Not exactly. Maybe if I knew more about what the increase covers. I picked up voice mails from a few unhappy citizens."

"We explained in the cover letter, but I can give you details. Hell, if you can appease Barbara Dougherty, we should hire you as community relations director. You obviously have a way with words."

She laughed, fighting an odd spike of excitement at the idea. "Like I said, we mostly talked about chiles." She took another bite. "Isn't there a desert foods cook-off in the festival? She should enter it."

"Talk to her about it," he said, rolling over her to brace himself on his elbows. "Look at you, making yourself at home—talking gardens with the town grouch, getting on the bowling team—"

She shoved a chip in his mouth to fight the warmth his words gave her. "Having an affair with the mayor."

"Ouch," he said. "There's that."

"It is nice, though," she said. "I don't usually fit in."

"What do you mean?"

"I'm kind of a loner, I guess." She'd always felt set apart. When she'd been a cocktail waitress, all the girls her age were college kids with bright futures, working for spending money. She'd felt like a loser. The lack of civilized pretense in strip clubs was a relief, but the ugly side of that world made her feel alienated. She had friends, but didn't really feel at home.

"Maybe you haven't found a place you want to fit in," he said softly. "Maybe you had things to figure out first."

"Maybe," she said, feeling too happy to ponder the idea. She snuggled against him.

"Sleepy?" he asked her.

"I should drive you home soon."

"In a bit." He tightened his arms around her and it felt so good it made her nervous.

"We've got this under control, right?" she said, to reassure them both. "We're not acting like Mark and Jasmine."

"We just screwed in the bowling alley, Autumn."

"And while I was driving. This is bad, isn't it?" She pushed up to look down at him, alarmed.

"We're taking a break," he said, trying to reassure her—and himself, she could tell by the tension in his face. "Me from my life. You from school. It's new. We got carried away."

"You're worried, aren't you?" she asked.

"A little. It was tough getting any work done today."

"So, how can I help you? To make up for my distracting you so much."

"Keep up with Lydia's work and that's plenty."

"But how can I take some of the pressure from you?"

"I don't know. It's mostly the festival. The committee chairs are spending too much. I've got to rein them in."

"Wouldn't Lydia have done that?"

"Maybe. But you don't know any of these people."

"That makes it easier to be the bad cop. Let me help you."

"I don't know, Autumn—"

"You can't do everything, Mike, even with tights and a cape and a big *S* on your chest." She traced the shape with her nail.

"True." He seemed pleased she'd pushed him. "You are a remarkable woman, Autumn. Wise and tough and strong and smart."

"See that you put that in my evaluation, Mr. Mayor." His words lit a glow inside her that embarrassed her.

He didn't smile at her joke. Instead, he looked at her

with an emotion as hot and strong as espresso. An emotion she wanted to warm her hands before.

She had the awful awareness that, despite her plans and all her rules, she'd slipped into the deep end after all.

10

THE NEXT WEEK PASSED IN A BLUR of work and sex and bowling. *Bowling.* Autumn couldn't believe she was throwing balls down the lane as if her life depended on it, and she was having fun doing it.

Of course there were the stolen moments in the ladies' room—they never risked full sex again, just mad kissing to sustain themselves through the hours until they could be alone again. Maybe that was what gave bowling its erotic edge.

She'd just finished her second week on the job and she felt more comfortable every day—with Mike, with the work and with the town.

All the great sex had lifted her onto her own version of Jasmine's pink cloud, but she was too happy to let that trouble her.

She liked that people greeted her by name at the diner, on the sidewalk or when she pulled out of the driveway in the morning. She had talked Barbara into entering the desert cook-off and every other day the woman brought her another salsa to sample.

Eric Sands, the mechanic across the street, had promised to look at Jasmine's engine. And Winnie Scranton, her neighbor on the other side, had brought a welcome basket of jalapeño-zucchini bread and four-cheese lasagna—recipes included—along with a jug of prickly pear margarita mix from Cactus Confections, which made her smile, reminding her of her friends Esmeralda and Sugar and their yearly birthday celebration.

In the week since she'd wrestled the assignment of dealing with the festival committee chairs from Mike, she'd contacted everyone except Celia, who'd proved elusive, worked over the details and suggested cost-cutting ideas, which had been mostly well-received. Mike insisted on touching base with everyone— backing her play, he claimed, but she knew he had a hard time delegating work, so she didn't take it personally.

She was doing damn good on the job. She'd made a couple of mistakes on invoices, but rectified them, and only had to call Lydia twice with questions. Lydia had promised to bring the baby into town hall one day soon so they could meet in person.

It was early Saturday evening and she lay with Mike in his big, soft bed. Mark and Jasmine were due back from Family Day at Cactus Ranch in a bit. Neither Autumn nor Mike had made headway with the pair, who now had dragged Sabrina into their entanglement.

Autumn had asked Jasmine to give her a heads-up about their return so she could hear how the camp visit went. It would also give her time to escape Mike's house before Mark returned.

For now, she was happy to lie in Mike's arms.

"This getting a life is pretty great," Mike said, rolling over onto her body.

"You'll have to keep it up after I go." But her words landed wrong, like a sour note, and she felt awful. Mike stilled.

Neither of them needed a reminder that she was leaving. She'd locked her doubts behind a steel door, just as she backed away from her game face to strip.

Mike seemed to want to ignore the tense moment. He ran his hands down her abdomen. "You have an incredible body."

"I have to add some miles to my runs since I've been eating all Barbara's salsa samples."

He chuckled. "You know that woman actually smiled at me in the post office yesterday?"

"That's because I told her how much you worry about the town—how you're up all night pondering the issues."

"When I'm really making love to you," he growled.

"Lately, sure, but it's true. You live and breathe Copper Corners and she should know that. Everyone should."

He cuddled her close to him. "You do so much for me, Autumn. What can I do for you?" His eyes searched her face.

"You're doing just fine," she breathed, running her fingers down the line of hair that led to his ready erection.

"I think I can do better. Hang on." He leaned down and circled her nipple with his tongue, then gave her a mischievous look. "Don't move." He left the bed and the room.

When he returned a few seconds later, he had something behind his back. "Close your eyes, Autumn."

She did, but squinted.

"No peeking."

"Mike—"

"Don't you trust me?"

"Sure," she said, "but—"

"I could tie you up and blindfold you."

"Okay." She relaxed her lids and waited, listening to him pad closer, feeling the mattress sink under his weight. His hip was warm against her body.

"You're still tense. Relax." He ran his tongue down the middle of her belly, almost to her spot.

She couldn't help but do what he asked. She stretched out, giving herself over to his tongue and hands, to whatever he wanted to do to her. She just let go.

Squirt. An icy blob of something hit her breast. She gasped and opened her eyes. "What are you…?" He'd made a circle of whipped cream around her nipple.

"Feel good?" He dosed her other breast.

"No…I mean…yes. Kind of." There was a flash of cold, then warm wet. Mmm.

Squirt. A line down her belly. *Squirt, squirt, squirt.* A triangle over her pubic area.

"Whipped cream bikini," Mike declared, lowering his head to lick one nipple, then the other.

"Oh. My." She lay there and enjoyed the experience as he ate his way across her breasts and down her belly to her spot, where he gripped her hips and hefted her up to his mouth.

"Very nice, but I prefer how you taste." His tongue reached her clit, electrifying her. "You like that?"

"Yyyeeesss."

"Or this?" He burrowed in, his nose working her.

"That. Oh, yes. And that. I like that. I like it all."

He added some cream and the jolt of chill contrasted with his hot tongue, until she was helplessly quivering under his onslaught of cream and tongue and touch.

Mike made love to her as if he had all the time in the world and she was the most important thing in it.

She would never get enough of him. She didn't want to think about what she would do when her internship was over and she had to go back to Phoenix.

I will miss you so much. The thought filled her mind and wouldn't fade, even while she took a turn with the whipped cream on Mike.

They were resting, sticky and laughing, when Jasmine called to say she and Mark were nearly home, so Autumn headed to the Huffmans' to await her friend's arrival.

She decided to prepare some snacks using the welcome basket. A batch of prickly pear margaritas seemed perfect, though it made her remember Esmeralda's psychic predictions about the changes Autumn supposedly would experience. *In heart and home and hearth. And heart shall lead.*

Crazy, she thought, pouring the tequila into the blender. She almost didn't hear her cell phone for the grinding ice. "Hello?" she said.

"You're doing it, hon." She recognized Esmeralda's musical voice. "Stop it."

"Hello, Esmie," she said, her heart lifting. "I was just thinking about you."

"Of course you were. I was prompted to call you."

"Must have been the smell of the prickly pear margaritas I'm blending wafting your way. Now what is it I'm supposed to stop doing?"

"Kicking your heart to the curb, sweets. Just don't."

"I'm not, Esmie." She shoved the margarita-filled blender container into the freezer to wait for Jasmine's arrival. "At least I don't think I am." She leaned against the refrigerator and sighed. "There *is* a guy. We're having a summer thing."

"But you don't want it to end."

"It has to. I have the revue and school and he's the mayor of this puny town and—"

"That's coming from your head, not your heart, Autumn."

"There's nothing wrong with that. My head's what's got me where I am."

"You don't have to wrestle happiness to the ground, Autumn. Sometimes it just comes to you."

There it was, Esmeralda's optimism. To Autumn it felt like a foreign language. But a secret part of her warmed to it, like the cats soaking up a patch of morning sun. "So how are you doing? How's the new job?" Esmeralda would be taking over the Dream A Little Dream Foundation. She'd gotten the job because of her psychic abilities.

"I start tomorrow. I'm excited and a little nervous. I don't have much business experience."

"They wouldn't hire you if they didn't think you could handle it. It's helping people like you always do, but with money this time, right?"

"Right. I just…I just want to do it right, no mistakes."

"How come you can be sure about me and so doubtful about you?"

"The eternal question of my life. My cosmic lesson."

"I know you'll do fine, Esmie. Any sign of your ex?"

"Not yet. I expect him any day, though." Esmie's birthday reading had indicated a man from her past would return. Not that Autumn bought all that, but there was Sugar to consider. "Have you talked to Sugar lately?"

"A week ago. She's deliriously happy. But she had to stand still and let her happiness in. Along with Gage. Call her. You're too much like her for your own good."

"Maybe I'll call." But she doubted that would help. She'd always taken comfort that, like her, Sugar didn't think she had the happily-ever-after gene. They used to laugh about it. Now Sugar had changed.

An ache started deep within Autumn, an *I want that* longing that would do no good whatsoever. She had to focus on what she and Mike had—an incredibly powerful sexual bond. She would make the most of this summer adventure. There was no point hoping for more.

"Ah, Autumn. You're doing it again."

"My heart is fine." She studied her bare index fingernail. "When I get back, will you do my nails again? One of my stars fell off and I miss it."

"Of course. I'm here for you, Autumn. Always remember."

"I never forget. And you'll do great with your job." She felt a tightening in her throat hearing her friend cheering for her.

"And remember to give him the benefit of the doubt. Consider the shades of gray."

"I'll be hanging up now before you threaten me with bird entrails or warn me against the Ides of March."

Esmie's musical laugh stayed in her ears. When she hung up, she found the cats swirling around her legs. "You hungry, guys?" But there was food in their bowl.

She kneeled down and Mocha scrubbed his furry cheek against her calf, while Marmalade touched her nose to Autumn's forehead. They wanted *her,* not food. Not so self-sufficient, after all. Hmm. Maybe she wasn't either. She felt better after hearing from her friend.

Before she started laying out the snacks, she checked on the other pets. The biggest angelfish seemed to perk up when it saw her and the turtle turned her way when she approached the terrarium. The chuckwalla scampered close to the glass. "Hey, Chuck. Miss me?" Kiwi-seed brain or not, there seemed to be some reaction going on.

She was caught up in Esmeralda's mysticism. Getting attached to the pets, the house, the town, the job.

To Mike.

Still, it was comforting having the cats watch her from side-by-side bar stools while she laid out slices of jalapeño-zucchini bread, chips and salsa for Jasmine, whose car was rumbling into the driveway this minute.

She had to remember to tell her about Eric the mechanic across the street.

When Jasmine walked in, Autumn held out a margarita glass. "Welcome home!"

"Wow," Jasmine said as she took the glass, then looked at the snack tray. "You cooked for me? How domestic."

"I made margaritas. That's festive, not domestic. And the neighbors made the food." Autumn explained who'd made what.

"I can't believe you know the neighbors, Autumn." Jasmine shooed Mocha from a bar stool and sat down. "What's this?" She picked up one of the two golf shirts sitting on the kitchen bar.

"I'm helping Evelyn with the decals for our bowling team."

"You're on a bowling team?" She looked startled.

"It's kind of part of my job." Autumn shrugged, then lifted Marmalade from the stool so she could sit, too, pleased when the cat turned and jumped onto her lap. Mocha jumped up, too, which made her heart tight with joy.

"At least the cats have been around." Jasmine looked sad. "I'm sorry I haven't been keeping you company."

"It's fine. I've been busy. With, um, town business." Lord, was her face flaming red? "So, how did it go at camp?"

"Great, in the end. It started out bad." Jasmine sipped her margarita, shaking her head. "We found Sabrina in the craft cabin and she gave us the stony stare. You know the one I mean?"

"Oh, yeah." Sabrina could imitate concrete if she wanted.

"So, she and I walked outside and she lit into me. 'Why are you ruining my camp? I have enough trouble reading a frickin' compass without having to deal with you and another lame boyfriend. Where did you meet that loser?' On and on."

"Sounds unpleasant." Autumn sipped her drink, running her fingers through the cats' fur, soothed by their purrs.

"Very. But I practiced reflective listening and when Sabbie finally finished, I calmly explained that I understood her concerns, but that Mark was different. One," Jasmine counted on her fingers, "he has a regular job. Two, no motorcycle or tattoos. Three, no bad habits. Four, he has a good heart. And five—" she pinched her thumb "—most important of all, he loves me to pieces."

"What did Sabrina say?"

"She did her Auntie Autumn imitation, of course. She rolled her eyes and told me she'd heard this all before."

"What did you say to that?"

"I was just about to start yelling at her when Mark came out with something he'd made. You know those plastic strips for lanyards? Well, he'd made a hammock for her Bratz doll and gave it to her. She was all, 'no thanks, I don't want that,' but I could tell she liked it."

"Then what happened?"

"I started to smooth it over, saying we should all just get along when—" She glanced at Autumn. "Don't give me that look. Someone has to see the silver lining, Princess Dark Cloud. But Mark put a hand on my arm and said, 'Sweetheart, Sabrina's not buying it.'"

"Good for him."

"Sabrina kind of smiled. Then Mark explained about how he hated B.S., too, when he was her age, and how he'd lost his parents and despised that adults always got all fake cheerful because they were freaked by his sadness. And then he said—"

Here Jasmine swallowed and Autumn saw there were tears in her eyes. "I promised myself I wouldn't cry." She drank more margarita. "Then he said, 'I love your mother with all my heart and I know you do, too, so maybe it'll rub off on us and we'll get to like each other some. After a while, I mean. No rush.'"

"That's very sweet." Her own throat tightened with emotion.

"Sabrina didn't say anything at first. She just looked down. And Mark said, 'If I get enough of this plastic stuff, you think I could make a whole dollhouse?'"

"Sabrina laughed, I bet."

"Yeah. But mainly she just looked at him. Then he said he'd heard there were family canoe rides and asked if she would go with us if he promised not to tip the boat over. So we paddled around the creek a while and the two of them joked. When we left Sabrina was happy."

"Happy?"

"Okay, Ms. Glass-Half-Empty. She said she didn't *hate* him and that I didn't ruin camp. And of course she had to tell me to not wreck it this time. Sometimes that girl is worse than you."

"She loves you and she worries."

"Like you. I get that. But the truth is, when I was there with Mark and Sabrina out in the water in that canoe, our laughter echoing against the canyon walls, I felt like we were a family. I was like a regular wife and a mother, not a stripper and a single mom and a divorcée and all the hard things."

"There's nothing wrong with being a stripper or a single mom. Lots of so-called happy families are miserable, Jas."

"I know that. But I have my dreams. I get lonely. So do you. You just pretend to like it."

"I don't pretend. I just know not to get myself into things that hurt too much getting out of."

"You can't win if you don't play."

"You can't go broke, either."

"What are you so afraid of, Autumn?"

"I'm afraid for you. I don't want to rain on your sunny day, but you two live in different worlds."

"Yeah, but—"

"Don't say 'love makes all things possible' again."

Her heart squeezed with worry for her friend, who was sinking deeper into emotional danger. Mark was a nice guy and maybe Sabrina liked him, but reality was still reality. "I don't want to upset you, but Mark doesn't always use good judgment. You know he went crazy for a married woman who was pure trouble."

"You mean Brenda? Mark told me all about her. That was different."

"You keep saying that."

"I'm different, too. Don't you think I can learn about myself and be stronger and smarter?"

"Sure you can. But it takes time to know a person."

Except she noticed that Jasmine *was* different. Her face was relaxed, her eyes warm. She seemed solid in her skin, not jittery, not tense, not even dreamy.

Or had being with Mike colored Autumn's world pink, too?

"Are you okay?" Jasmine said. "You look spaced out."

"I'm fine. Just worried about you."

"But not so much? You can see I do know what I'm doing?"

"Maybe. I hope this works out for you.

She leaned closer, studying Autumn. "You have a goofy look on your face and you're petting those cats like they're yours. And what's this?" She leaned down and picked up something from the floor—Autumn's open-nipple bra, which Mike had torn off her the other night.

"One of the cats, I guess." She grabbed it from Jasmine and balled it up. "Want a refresher?" She headed for the freezer, aware of Jasmine's eyes on her back.

"Grab more ice. This is kind of strong."

Autumn added ice, then ran the blender, while

Jasmine said something about the pageant and Nevada and choreography. Autumn couldn't hear clearly. She was just relieved that Jasmine hadn't detected her secret.

She handed the watered-down margarita to Jasmine, who said, "So, what do you think about that? Isn't it cool?"

"Cool? Uh…" She was about to ask for clarification when her cell phone, resting on the counter, went off. It had to be Mike and she felt heat rise to her cheeks. "Hello?" she said, hoping her voice didn't shake.

"Hey, gorgeous. What are you wearing?" Her stomach plunged with the pleasure of hearing his voice and the sexy thing he'd said. Luckily, Jasmine was focused on the snacks.

"I'm fine. Yes, I'll be in at nine on Monday."

"Jasmine's there?" he asked.

"Yes, that's right," she said, catching Jasmine's eye and indicating she was leaving the room to take the call. "I finished the notes as you requested."

"Think about it," Jasmine called to her as she walked away.

"Sure," she called back, having no idea what Jasmine had asked her about the pageant and not caring with Mike's voice in her ear. "Same thing I was wearing when I left you," she whispered when she reached her room and closed the door.

"How about I sneak over and take it off again?"

She closed her eyes with the rush his words gave her. "Too risky. Jasmine's sleeping here tonight."

He sighed. "Tomorrow then."

"It sounds so far away." She felt desperate to see him.

"I know. I want my tongue on you." He spoke so low and sexy she could hardly bear it. Her body turned to liquid.

"You do?" She lay on her bed, her heart pounding, burning for him, wanting him so much. Esmie was wrong about her heart. It wasn't on the curb, it was aching like mad.

"I want to taste your skin…I want to taste you."

"That sounds so good."

"I can hear it in your voice. I can see you in my mind. You're licking your lips, aren't you?"

She stopped mid-lick. "How did you know?"

"I know you. When you start to get aroused you close your eyes a little and lick your lips real slow. It's very hot."

"I didn't realize that." But she was doing it again.

"Yeah. Why don't you get naked and I'll talk you through what I'd do if I were there with you?"

Phone sex. "You have the best ideas," she said.

In seconds, she was naked on the bed, open to the air and Mike's whispered words, urging her to touch herself for him. "You're wet and so slick, aren't you?"

"Mmm-hmm."

"I want to be there. I want to touch you."

"I want you here," she breathed.

"I can see your hips moving. Your head is back…you're so beautiful. You get this light in your face. It's like nothing I've seen and I want to keep seeing it."

She couldn't speak. She was captive to his voice, to his low commands, to his desire for her.

Her body tightened into a climax just as she heard the harsh breathing that told her he was coming, too.

This was so good. How could she expect more?

This pleasure they shared was wonderful. It was plenty. It was enough. Any more would be just plain greedy.

A FEW NIGHTS LATER, Autumn rested her head on Mike's chest and ran her fingers lazily along the curves of his chest muscles, happily exhausted.

After the phone sex, she'd rededicated herself to the sexual adventure they were enjoying together and they'd tried several different positions to mind-bending effect. Now she was worn out, her limbs heavy and her mind sluggish.

"Maybe we should do something outside," Mike said lazily, running his fingers through her hair. She loved that.

"You mean on the golf course again?"

"I mean something besides sex."

"But that's what we do, Mike." She rolled over and braced her chin on his chest. "That's our thing."

"I was thinking we could go hang gliding."

She laughed, assuming he was kidding.

"You'd like it. Come on, seize the day. I'm trying to learn from you."

"We don't have time with the festival coming up, do we?"

"We could slip it in. Next Saturday, maybe?"

"I don't know. Listen, don't forget to fill out the evaluation from my program advisor."

"Draft something for me and I'll sign it." He yawned.

She pushed up from his chest. "*You* have to evaluate me, Mike, and it has to be honest. The internship's almost over and if there's something I'm not doing, I—"

"You're doing great, Autumn. No worries."

"Okay, then." She fell back on the bed and he cuddled her close.

"You know, small towns need accountants, too."

She froze.

"Maybe we could squeeze out a town salary for you, if we worked over the budget. Or there's Ben Godwin, who does taxes for lots of folks. He's about to retire."

She pushed up again and looked down at him. "Mike, that's nice of you, but we're just... We're together for my internship. I've got school and a job in Phoenix."

"I know that," he said, his eyes searching hers. "I like spending time with you. Maybe we could stay in touch, you know?"

Her heart lodged in her throat. This was just what she feared, making too much of a summer thing. "It's always hard to come back from vacation. Let's not make more of this than there could ever be."

He was silent for a long time, looking at her. Finally, he exhaled. "You're probably right."

She was surprised at how sad she felt, how his wish for more stayed in her head. She shivered, confused and lost.

"You cold?" He pulled the sheets up over her, then kissed her gently on the top of the head.

She had *plans*. Get her degree, get a good job, get experience, network. In three years, maybe less, she'd have enough contacts to open her own firm. She'd promised Nevada and Jasmine two more years with the revue, too, maybe more to sock away money for her business. She'd worked it all out. She had a plan. No way was her future in tiny Copper Corners, Arizona.

But Mike wanted more.

But Mike didn't even know her. He had this picture

of her as a plucky little cocktail waitress saving her pennies to go to college.

If he knew who she was—what she was—he'd see how impossible it would be to want something more with her. Even better, she would see, too. What they both needed was a reality check. A reality check would fix everything.

11

DON'T WRECK THIS, *you ass,* Mike told himself, watching Autumn sleep. *She's temporary, like the job. She's got school and a life you know nothing about.*

He pushed her hair from her cheek and felt so much tenderness he didn't know how to contain it.

He was like a kid at Disneyland throwing a tantrum when it was time to leave. The park had to close sometime. In fact, that was part of the magic. They could exhaust themselves on the rides, eat too many churros and red vines and push through the exit turnstile, content they'd enjoyed every moment until they locked the gates.

Except…look at her. He watched the moonlight play on her cheeks. In sleep, her face was as innocent as a child's.

She made him feel like a kid himself, the way he'd felt before his parents died, when the world was easy to take and every surprise was a happy one, when he didn't have to be on guard every minute to keep something vital from crashing, cracking, falling apart or dying.

He liked Autumn's level head, but he loved her sensitive heart, which she protected with her cynicism. What had she said about not wanting a boyfriend or a husband? *Being alone is better.* No. She meant *safer*. It was like she didn't dare hope.

He shared her practicality, but not her pessimism. Happiness was possible. A good marriage and a life full of love was not a miracle. It was within reach. And he wanted that.

With Autumn? The idea jumped inside him like a hot spark he immediately doused.

Wouldn't work. For one thing, she wasn't interested. She'd never move here and he'd never leave Copper Corners. Managing an affair had been tough enough. Work was piling up. His mayoral duties and even the festival planning now seemed like so much static—a radio off its station.

He'd let her tilt his world on its side. Which made him wonder how realistic he was about his plan to settle down. Would a wife or even a girlfriend put up with his devotion to the town? How would he establish balance?

Of course, the woman he'd choose probably wouldn't throw him into a tailspin the way Autumn had. Maybe that was the lesson. Have an affair with a wild woman, but when it came time to choose a mate, pick someone sensible.

Either way, he had some thinking to do.

At least he knew that. He was being reasonable. Unlike his brother, who was ready to run away with his stripper girlfriend. Mike had heard bizarre rumors about where the two had done the deed, in the covered wagon on stage—which was true—at one of Mark's For-Sale properties, and on the roof of the pool hall, which he couldn't imagine since the surface was patched with sun-sticky tar.

He checked the clock. 2:00 a.m. He'd lost hours somehow. When he was with Autumn, time zoomed by.

Now she was a naked angel shining up at him in the dark. He thought about the suits she wore over her wild underwear. It was as though she had a split personality— sober and serious on the outside, dead sexy underneath.

She wasn't so sure about that outside self, he knew, so he wrapped his body around her, imagining himself as her shield against doubts. He wanted her to leave here feeling invincible.

He cared about her, but it wasn't love. You didn't fall in love in two weeks. The fact he even considered it was a big fat caution sign he'd damn well better heed.

Except, early the next morning when he kissed her awake and she smiled up at him, unguarded, open and warm, something in his heart broke off and floated away, flooding through him. Something warm and good and right.

As she steadied herself, grew alert, he watched her withdraw from him. *Small towns need accountants, too.* Shit. Why had he said that?

She hid in his backseat so he could sneak her home, but didn't reach for him the way she usually did. He'd opened his big mouth and ruined things between them.

He parked in the alley behind her house and she jumped out.

"You're forgetting something," he said, calling her back for their usual tease, trying to make things normal again.

She returned, forcing a smile. "How about the peach lace?"

"You got something I haven't seen yet?"

She looked in at him and he could see that she wanted to go back to how they'd been, too. "Not really." A wicked spark lit in her eyes. She made her fingers into scissors and pretended to snip away. "I'll make the panties crotchless."

"Oh, yeah."

She dashed off, leaving him dizzy with the image of her open to his fingers under her business suit. He had to sit for a bit before he could see to drive.

She was back with him. At least that.

MIKE WAS TALKING to Evelyn when Autumn entered town hall a few hours later, to-go cup in hand, wearing her navy blue suit.

And cut-open panties. He stopped in the middle of a sentence to stare. Realizing Evelyn was watching, he jerked his eyes to the overhead clock and frowned so he'd seem serious.

"That clock is fast," Evelyn said quickly. "She's actually five minutes early."

"Let's get it fixed." He cleared his throat, grateful for his accidental cover. "Could I see you in my office?" he said to Autumn. He had to touch her.

By the time she left his office, he was in a haze. What was he doing, fooling around in town hall? He was the mayor, for God's sake.

Evelyn buzzed through on the intercom. "Your brother's on line one. Listen, I don't know what you said to her, but poor Autumn was trembling like a leaf when she came out. Don't be so hard on her."

But she likes it hard. He almost laughed at the thought. "I'll try to do better." He'd rather Evelyn think he was being tough on Autumn than that he was insanely caught up in an affair with her.

He pushed the button for line one and said hello to Mark.

"Hey, bro. So I hear you're browbeating the staff."

"What?"

"Evelyn said you're hassling Autumn."

"Autumn's doing fine." *And just the sound of her name makes me want her.*

"Are you sure? You sound odd."

"I'm sure. She's fine. What's up?"

"We need you to come to a rehearsal for the pageant. We've made some changes and need you to okay it."

"Some changes?"

"Yeah. We'll do a dress rehearsal of the new sections for you. Next week."

"Okay, I guess. I'm pretty swamped with the festival." Mostly, he didn't want to lose a moment of time with Autumn.

"So delegate some work."

"No one's stepping up to the plate, Mark."

"That's because when they do, you jam your mitt in front yelling, 'I got it. I got it.' Let go a little, Mike. You deserve a personal life."

"I do fine." He had a personal life right now he didn't dare talk about. He and Autumn weren't far from knocking over covered wagons themselves. "Besides, there's such a thing as letting too much go. I'm hearing rumors about you two going at it all over town."

Mark chuckled. "Don't believe everything you hear. Well, believe some of it. The open house was over. I just forgot I'd left the lock box on."

"Good Lord."

"It's just so good, Mike. I can't even say."

"You're still planning to go to Phoenix?"

"I am. It's right."

"It's just that—you don't fall in love that fast.

Maybe the sex is great, but you need to be compatible, to want the same things, to agree on—"

"Dammit, Mike, would you chill out?" Mark's anger made him realize he'd been giving the lecture he meant for himself.

"Sorry. Guess the stress is getting to me," he mumbled.

"Jeez. I guess so. Look, no one's indispensable. The world turns fine without you supervising the angle, speed and torque."

"I know that. I just—" He still wanted to look out for Mark if he could. "Do me a favor, would you? Don't close Fields Real Estate right away. See how it goes?" At least if the Jasmine thing fell apart, Mark would have his business waiting for him when he came back.

"You never stop, do you?" Mark said. "Okay. I'll consider it. Whatever happened with that dating service? You need to get out more, get laid, I don't know. Something."

"I'm fine. Trust me."

AUTUMN'S HEART WAS A KNOT of tension as she drove home with Mike hidden in her backseat. They'd had fun with the cut-out panties at work, but things would never be the same again after what Mike had suggested.

She knew what she had to do. And it would probably end their affair. How long could they sustain things at this level, anyway, right?

Inside the garage, she rushed straight for the door instead of pausing to kiss Mike as they usually did. "Wait for me in the living room," she said to him over her shoulder.

"Okay." Mike sounded puzzled. He'd been trying all day to pretend nothing had happened, but everything was different now.

At the entertainment center, she turned on the CD player very loud and went to her room to dress.

She'd decided on a simple look: black bikini top, black thong, black stockings and black office pumps—as close to stilettos as she'd brought to Copper Corners. In the mirror, she looked fine, but she felt strange. Instead of feeling fiercely sexy, she felt shaky and uncertain.

Ridiculous. She closed her eyes, steadied herself, then looked again. Much better. *Game face on. Soul tucked away.*

She was a stripper, a sexual artist, and a damned good one. Mike would be shocked, of course. No way would the mayor of Copper Corners want to date a stripper, even in secret. There was more to her than met the eye and it was about time he saw.

Rock and roll.

"Music's kind of loud!" he called to her.

"Leave it!" she shouted back. She needed it that way because that's how it was in the club and she needed to drown out her doubts.

She straightened her spine, stood with her legs wide and when the Stones tune "Start Me Up" kicked off, she did her best strut into the living room.

"Wow," Mike said when he saw her, rising to his feet.

"Stay there," she said firmly, hand up to stop him.

He sat, grinning. He thought she was playing a sex game. Not this time.

She strode close, then swung her hips into a slow turn with a full body roll, then faced him.

"You look good. That is hot." He looked stunned and turned on at the same time.

Her heart ached. She had to think of him as just another customer in for the Businessman's Lunch. Roast beef, potato salad and a hard-on to go.

But this was *Mike*. His eyes had adored her, his hands had touched her tenderly.

You know, small towns need accountants, too.

She danced away from him to the low wall between the living room and dining room, concentrating on her moves. She slid into a squat, arms high, as if holding a pole, legs wide.

She felt sick inside, which was stupid. She wasn't ashamed of what she did. Not at all.

She rose, then turned to bend over, rocking her backside for his pleasure, then turned and danced closer. She was rushing her moves, but she was more nervous than she'd expected to be, sweating and shaky. She untied her top and dropped the cups, then stroked her breasts, teasing her nipples, her hips doing an erotic glide.

Mick Jagger on the CD shouted that he'd *never stop, never stop, never, never, never stop.* She untied the string at her back and tossed her top at Mike. It landed on his shirt, but he reached for her, his eyes eating her up.

"No touching." She wagged a finger at him.

He dropped his hands, but he wouldn't leave her alone long, she could tell, and her heart sped up. "Jasmine teach you this?" he asked, his voice husky. "Because you're good."

For just a blink of time, she considered saying yes, letting it be just a game, but she owed them both the truth.

"Jasmine didn't have to teach me," she said, looking

him square in the eye. "I already knew how. I'm a stripper. Just like she is." Feeling vulnerable, she crossed her arms over her breasts.

"You're a stripper? But you told me—"

"I *was* a waitress, but for the last ten years I've been stripping. Lots better money."

"Why didn't you tell me?" He looked so hurt that her game face dropped away completely. She felt raw.

"It didn't matter then."

"But it matters now?" He stood, pondering her words. "Why? Because of what I said last night?"

She didn't move or speak. She just hugged herself.

Mike's face took on the same look as it had had before she spoke. He didn't seem that shocked, really, and he certainly wasn't disgusted.

"You're telling me this because you want...what?" He stepped toward her.

"I want you to know who I really am." She backed up.

"I already do." He stepped closer.

She shook her head. Didn't he get it? "I take off my clothes for men, Mike." He was too close and she couldn't catch a free breath. She stepped back again.

He moved in. "I get that," he said.

"I deliberately turn them on. I do lap dances." She backed up again, but he kept coming, his gaze steady, telling her it didn't matter.

"Lately, we've been doing burlesque, which involves less nudity, but I'm still a stripper. Not a show girl or an exotic dancer. And I'm fine with that."

He seemed to see through her, as if her words were the business suit she'd covered herself with and he saw her to the bones.

She reached the wall and couldn't back up any

more. "So, you're shocked, right?" She had to get to the point, to the fact that they had to end things.

"Yeah, I'm shocked. And I'm pissed that you lied to me. But it doesn't change how I feel." He put his arms around her, pulling her away from the wall.

"I'm going back to the revue, Mike." She wanted to push him away, but his arms felt so good around her.

"I know that," he said, kissing her neck.

"This is just while I'm here."

"I know that, too," he said, kissing her mouth.

"Don't you get it? You're sleeping with a stripper. The mayor of Copper Corners hooked up with a—"

He stopped her with a kiss, but she forced herself out of his arms. "You're not listening to me, Mike. You're just horny and blind to everything but that."

"I heard every word." He pulled her to him, even though she put her hands between them. "I know you're scared," he said softly. "If you want to stop seeing me, say so."

She looked at him, her breath coming in harsh gasps, her heart surging with impossible emotions.

"Do you want to end this right now?" he asked again.

"No," she said.

"Good, because neither do I." He pulled her into his arms and the fight went out of her. She buried her face in his neck, happy and scared, and almost sure this was a mistake, but not caring at the moment. Her bare breasts felt good against the thick cotton of his shirt. She felt his heart thud, solid and sure, telling her it would be all right.

The sexy Stones song ended and a softer bluesy number began.

"This wasn't how this was supposed to go," she said, looking up at him.

"How was that?" He spread his fingers against her bare back, then slid to her bottom, bared by her thong.

"You're supposed to come to your senses."

He leaned to kiss her breast and slid a finger beneath the thong strip, along her sex, then into her. "So you had another life before you met me," he murmured. "So what?"

And now she'd leave it? But he was stroking her and she didn't want to think that he didn't really get it. She moaned and began to shake in his arms.

"Come for me, Autumn," he said. He slid a second finger inside, lifting her, catching her G-spot so she was helpless, pinned between his hands—one on her sex and sliding into her, the other stroking her bottom. "Come for me, baby."

"I can't stand up…."

"I'm holding you. I want you to let go."

"I can't…I can't…I can't."

"You can. You are."

The spasms overtook her, and she made wild sounds, gave up control, so glad he held her, his fingers still on her and in her. The waves passed through her like a continuous electric charge. Finally, she fell against his chest, weak from her release.

He held her, kissed her neck, her mouth, her face. "I want to be inside you," he said. Gently, he turned her, bent her over the soft leather of the sofa, then reached around to stroke her with one hand while he shifted the thong out of the way and slid into her.

At that angle, she felt every inch of his cock curving into her as her body stretched to welcome his length.

"I live to be inside you," he said and slowly pulled out, then in. Easy at first, in and out, deeper each time.

He held his finger on her clit so that she didn't need to move. She couldn't have anyway. He'd pinned her over the sofa, filling her body full of him. She couldn't do a thing, except feel the pressure of his cock, its gliding slide, the pinch of his finger on her clit, the rising rush of heat and need. She made a mewling sound.

"I know, baby. I know," he said. "I feel it, too." And then he sped up, pushing her climax up and over and they cried out together and lunged for the other side, her name on his lips, his on hers.

Hours later, they lay tangled in the sheets, naked, slippery with sweat, legs interlocked, the night bathing them in a silver glow.

"What are we doing, Mike?" she asked him, feeling as though she was in a dream.

"We're not walking away from this yet."

Mike knew about her other life and it hadn't ended their affair. Now she had the best of both worlds—no secrets and no promises.

12

WHEN AUTUMN STUCK HER HEAD into Mike's office on Friday, he was on the phone, but he motioned her in anyway. She knew they should stop doing this, even though they had the excuse of the festival, which, at only a week away, required lots of consultations. Of course, it also helped that Evelyn thought Autumn was in trouble with Mike.

We have a problem, he would say and frown and Autumn would hurry into his office. The *problem,* of course, was all the hours they had to wait before they'd be alone again.

A week had passed since she'd stripped for Mike and he seemed as happy as she was to stay in the moment, focused on sex, not discussing what would happen after the festival.

They'd set limits, at least, and were scrupulously discreet. They were using good sense. A lot of the appeal was how forbidden the affair was.

Maybe the end would seem natural and welcome. After all, how long could they sustain this intensity?

They were both behind at work, constantly distracting each other. They'd managed the bowling league games, but ducked out on practice with separate, reasonable excuses. Now she was in here keeping Mike from his duties again.

"And I'll meet you as soon as I can," Mike said to his caller. "Sure. Great." He hung up and smiled at her. "What have you got going right now?"

"The Daisy Mae—yellow, see-through bra and no panties whatsoever."

"Damn." He visibly winced at her words, his darling face going pink, his eyes smoky. She loved how he responded to every sexy thing she did. "I meant work-wise…though that's great news for later."

"I have to talk to Celia about the decorations budget. She's ducking my calls, so I'm going over to the shop."

"Bearding the lion in her den?"

"I figure if we borrow chairs from the churches, we won't have to rent them and that'll save some money."

"Excellent. And you're right to get Celia in person. She's good at ducking people. It feels like you've been here forever." He held her gaze, while seconds ticked by.

Sometimes she felt as if she almost belonged. It might be the relief of doing well. But she was pretty sure it was Mike. She'd never really fit anywhere and this seemed too easy, like a trick or a dream.

"Glad I'm helping."

"When you finish with Celia, could you do me a favor?"

"If you lock the door," she said, low and sexy.

"Mmm. Don't distract me." He shook his head, smiling, but clearly caught up in the idea. "Anyway…what was I saying? Oh, yeah. I've got to go over the newspaper ad with the publisher, but the carnival rides got here early because of a venue cancellation. I need you to meet the owner—Wayne Whittaker—at Desert Paradise. Make sure everything's there and sign off for me, okay?"

He handed her a folder. "The checklist's inside. I'll be out as soon as I can."

"No problem."

"Maybe we can pick up those golf balls afterward," he said, slipping his hand under her skirt to squeeze her thigh with possession and promise. At this angle, no one looking in his window could see anything amiss.

"Sounds fun," she murmured, bracing herself on his desk.

"Not as much fun as no underwear." He patted her and seemed to have to physically struggle to remove his hand.

"See you out there then." At his door, she blew him a kiss that he pretended to catch. So corny.

She didn't care. Corny was okay for Copper Corners.

Pushing into the Cut 'N Curl, Autumn was hit by a blast of hairspray and perfumed ammonia. The front of the shop held a cash register and a book rack labeled *Dr. Heidi's Advice* full of self-help and parenting books. The thought of Heidi made Autumn smile.

Farther into the shop, a young stylist worked on an older woman's white hair in the first of the two stations. The nail tech, also young, filed a pregnant woman's nails. Celia was busy with a weave on a long-haired brunette in the other chair. A fourth customer wore foil under one of the dryers.

"Hey, girl," Celia said, seeing her. "Sit your cute hiney down here and tell us what's up." She pointed at a stool beside the mirror. "I can squeeze you in for some highlights."

"That's okay."

"They'll make your color pop."

"Maybe one day. Right now I need to talk to you

about the festival decorations budget." She held out Celia's Swiss-cheese form on a clipboard.

"Autumn is standing in for Lydia," Celia explained to the customers, stylist and nail tech, who were all listening. "She's going to make me cut costs, I can feel it already."

"You're staying at the Huffmans', right?" said the white-haired woman, whose name was Raylene. "And your friend is making the costumes for the pageant?"

"That's right."

"We've never actually *hired* someone to do costumes before. I thought that was odd." Raylene pursed her lips. She had more to say that wouldn't be nice, Autumn could tell.

"Jasmine's an excellent designer," Autumn said.

"That's what I hear…." Raylene cut a look to the woman under the dryer.

"So I hope Mayor Mike's not breathing down your neck," Celia said to Autumn, clearly changing the subject. "Sometimes he acts like he's the only one who does anything in this town."

"He's a good mayor," said the woman under the dryer. "I wouldn't want the job."

"The man would wrestle anyone to the ground who tried to take it from him." Celia chuckled. "Mike's a dear. He just doesn't know when to stop."

"So, have you figured it out yet?" the nail tech, Jessica, asked Autumn.

"Figured what out?" Autumn asked.

"If he's gay?" Jessica asked the question as if it was too obvious to need repeating.

"That's rude, Jess," Celia said. She'd begun to cut Raylene's hair.

"The man goes to the opera. And he's never with a woman."

"I don't think he's gay," Autumn said, feeling her face flame.

"Not that there's anything wrong with that," Celia said, "if he were, I mean. Jeez-o-Pete."

"The cute ones always are." This from the nail client.

"You're about to have a baby, Delores."

"I'm married, not blind. Mayor Mike is hot."

"So, anyway, Celia," Autumn said, determined to get to the point, "could we talk about the budget?"

While Celia snipped, Autumn went over the figures, suggested cheaper street banners, recommended borrowing the church chairs and explained how a bulk order of paper table clothes would be less costly than laundering borrowed ones.

Celia agreed to her suggestions and even said yes when Autumn asked her to donate a makeover to the Children's Fund silent auction.

"That's it?" she asked when Autumn put away her pen. "That hardly hurt a bit. You're good. Want me to do those highlights?"

"No thanks, but I will use your restroom."

Celia nodded in the direction, but Autumn was in the room when she realized she'd left her lipstick in her purse on the stool and started back. She was just about to round the corner when she heard the woman under the dryer yell out, "Oh, yeah. Right on the stage, bold as you please, while the high school kids hammered on the stagecoach."

Autumn recognized the exaggerated tale and froze.

"At Yolanda's last night, I had to make my little granddaughter avert her eyes." Raylene's voice.

"So they made out," Celia said. "Are you forgetting how it is to be young and in love?"

"There's a time and a place for mauling each other."

"I heard they got caught doing it at one of the houses Mark's got up for sale." Jessica, she thought.

"More power to 'em." This from the pregnant woman. "Before I became a small country, me and Bill were like that."

"She's a *stripper*." Raylene again.

"Shush," someone said.

"The poor man," Raylene said. "She's likely a prostitute and a druggie. She has a kid, no less. Probably wants a sugar daddy."

"Don't be so quick to judge." Celia again. Autumn liked Celia more and more. "Mark's no idiot and she's a friend of Heidi's."

"I would hate for that sweet man to get hurt." Jessica sighed.

Autumn had had enough. She marched around the corner, hands on her hips. "My friend Jasmine is not a hooker and she doesn't do drugs. She handles her own finances and she loves her daughter with all her heart. Worry about your own sad lives and leave her alone, you…you…" Autumn's voice shook so she stopped short of calling them *small-minded bitches*.

"We're so sorry," Celia said. "Aren't we, ladies?"

The women had the decency to look stricken.

"Don't apologize to me. I don't give a shit what you think. Apologize to Jasmine and Mark. They're the ones you hurt."

She grabbed her purse and strode out of the shop, slamming the door so hard the glass rattled. Small towns and small minds. For every neighbor bringing a basket of cranberry-nut bread, there were three with binoculars and big mouths. For every sweet hello to your face, there were three jackknives in your back. She felt like crying.

Ridiculous. Who cared what they said in this little town? She should laugh about it, remember the stories for back at Moons. Of course she wanted to protect Jasmine. But Jasmine would soon leave this place in the dust of her Jetta, Mark in tow.

But I liked it here. That little whine high in her mind was why this stung. She'd had this strange, sweet feeling about the place, as if Copper Corners was the way family was supposed to be—comfortable and supportive and generous and accepting.

She knew better. Mike had changed her views.

Mike. What would those shrews say if they knew that only moments ago their beloved mayor had been feeling up a stripper? It boggled the mind.

She headed across the street to drop off Celia's budget before meeting the carnival guy.

When she entered the building, Evelyn looked up. "You smell like Celia's. Get your hair done?"

"No." And she would never darken that door again. In fact, she was still trembling with anger.

"Are you okay? Here. Drink." She held out her mug. "It's lemon ginseng tea."

Autumn took a sip of the tangy liquid, gripping the mug with both hands to hide how she shook. "Thanks, Evelyn."

"It's Quincy's favorite."

She glanced at the cat, hoping he hadn't sampled her cup, but not really caring.

"What happened?"

"Some mean comments about my friend Jasmine."

"Oh, hell's bells, don't let that get to you. That's beauty shop jujitsu, hon. Even good people go bad in there. Celia tries to keep a lid on it."

"I don't know why it bothered me so much." She'd endured plenty of gossip in high school. She'd handled it fine—shined it on, head high, ready with a zinger or a middle finger, depending on the mood and the creep she faced.

Her mother had stories, too. The neighbors once called the cops on her, claiming she was hooking out of her trailer. Her mother told the story to her with anger and defiance—*Those frigid freaks wouldn't know what to do with a healthy man if you gave 'em a manual*—but her eyes had been murky with pain.

Right now, helpless rage bubbled inside Autumn.

"It hurts, I know," Evelyn said. "That crowd decided my Karen drank during her pregnancy and that was why Kimmie has her learning problems. I wanted to tie 'em down and shave 'em bald, but you can't let the nasties get to you. Drink your tea. You're better than that. So are those women, for that matter. Maybe it's all the hairspray—makes 'em light-headed."

Evelyn insisted Autumn finish her tea before she left. Quincy eyed her mug the entire time. By the time she set out to meet Wayne Whittaker of Western Carnivals, she was calm but worried.

If the gossips at the Cut 'N Curl found out about her and Mike, he would suffer for it. It was bad enough his brother was running off with a stripper. Add Mike to the mix and the town would think the Field brothers had lost all sense.

Mike was clueless, caught up in the forbidden thrill of

it, oblivious to the repercussions of their fling. He was not prepared for the sneers, the doubts about his judgment.

She knew how it felt.

How much did you charge him for that blow job?

The question was from a cheerleader whose boy-friend had asked Autumn for math help. She'd been stunned, but managed to snap, *It was a freebie. I felt sorry for him. You need lessons, bitch.*

The injustice and shame still burned. She'd insulted herself more than the girl. The guy *had* hit on her and she'd said no. She never slept with guys who had girl-friends. She had strong values, but everyone believed her to be a slut and that was all that mattered.

She never wanted to feel that shame again. And she did not want Mike to have anything to live down. She had to talk to him, make him see what he risked. One of them had to be sensible.

BY THE TIME MIKE made it out to the Desert Paradise, the sun was dipping in the sky, sunset in the wings. He'd left Autumn to handle the carnival guy completely on her own. When he saw how late he'd be, he'd tried her cell, but the call went straight to voice mail.

He hoped there hadn't been complications. It was one thing to delegate duties, another to send someone out unprepared. She was a temp, for God's sake, and he'd been treating her like a deputy mayor.

He shook his head. What was happening to him? His brain buzzed and he felt dizzy half the time. The festival was a week away and he had to force himself to care. He hadn't made a single follow-up call on the business leads he'd gotten, there were three property line disputes he needed to mediate before things got ugly and a dozen action items from the last council meeting he hadn't touched.

And he still had this insane hope that he and Autumn could fit in a hang glider flight.

He'd get back his focus eventually. After Autumn left. That was the shoe waiting to drop. Their relationship was as temporary as her job. And he didn't know what to do about it—push for more or let it end when she left. He knew without asking her that she'd want it to end.

The resort parking lot held six carnival semis and Autumn's little Subaru. At first he didn't see her, then he noticed someone lying on a plastic bench under a tree beside the kiddie Ferris wheel, the only ride that had been assembled. The others were scattered around the resort grounds under tarps.

He saw she'd rested her head on her jacket and purse. Her feet were bare. There was no one else around. "Hey, there," he said when he stood over her.

"Hey, yourself." She smiled up at him in the dusk light, then sat up.

"Sorry I'm so late." He sat beside her. "Everything go okay? I got voice mail when I called your cell."

"The battery ran out. I decided just to wait for you—and the sunset. Look." She indicated the distant horizon where the sky was streaked with clouds of pink and orange.

"Gorgeous." He turned to her and fought the usual impulse to hold her tight, kiss her, smell her hair, for God's sake. It was as if he didn't believe his good fortune unless he actually had her in his arms.

"Wait'll you hear my news." Her eyes shone at him.

You love me and can't live without me? His heart rose with the ridiculous hope of it. "Tell me."

"The carnival guy is interested in the Desert Paradise!"

"That's amazing." Though, he realized, not as amazing as what he'd wished she'd said. "How'd it happen?"

"I suggested he wait for you and we started chatting. He mentioned that the carnival business had become erratic, that he wanted a quiet place to retire. He noticed all the golf balls and asked me about the course and I told him how much potential the resort had. He likes the desert."

"You're kidding me."

"Would I kid about Copper Corners's economic growth? I borrowed his phone and called Mark and he's going to show him the property tomorrow."

"So, basically, in your spare time you pitched the resort?"

"You better make me an honorary member of your economic development committee, huh? Put it on my evaluation."

"You're amazing." He leaned in to kiss her, but she pushed to her feet.

"How about a ride on the Ferris wheel?"

"What?"

She slid into her sandals, then tugged his hand. "Come on. I worked at a kiddie land one summer. Plus, Wayne told me where the keys are."

He went with her to the low fence, which she unlatched, then she took a large keychain from a metal box under the control station. "It's not hang gliding, but it's something. Get in the bottom car and I'll start it and jump on."

"Are you nuts?"

"We used to do this after the park closed all the time. Go on!"

How could he argue when she looked at him that way? He ran to the brightly painted seat and climbed in. Autumn engaged the machinery and his chair rose slowly clockwise. When it came around to the ground again, she boosted herself into the seat.

"Isn't this fun?" She stretched her toes against the metal footrest, ignoring the safety bar altogether.

"Yeah." God, he cared about her.

They made the slow turn, rising into the sky like Mike's heart and his hope.

"Sunset and a carnival," she said at the top. "Don't you love it?" He'd never heard her voice sound so soft.

He looked out at the vivid blue of the dusk sky, the pink clouds sliding by, wispy as cotton candy, at the lights coming up on his town in the distance. Then he looked at Autumn—her strong green eyes, soft mouth, hair a deep copper in the dimming light. "Yeah, I do." He put his arm around her and leaned in to kiss her.

She leaned away. "Not here. It's not worth the risk."

"We're alone," he said.

"In a small town, you're never alone. I just got a big fat reminder today at the Cut 'N Curl where a bunch of nasty women accused Jasmine of being a hooker and an addict who wants Mark as a sugar daddy."

"Oh, for God's sake." Anger shot through him. "It's that damned beauty shop. Who were the women? I'll talk to them."

"It's not the shop. It's small towns. It's how it is. It's—"

"I'll talk to Celia."

"What do you expect, Mike? Jasmine's a stripper. So am I, and if the citizens of Copper Corners knew you were sleeping with me, they'd go nuts."

"It's no one's business who I date."

"We're not dating, Mike, remember? We're screwing." Her words were hard and she retreated behind the armor of them.

"It's more than that and you know it. I don't care what anyone says."

"Yes, you do. Your reputation matters to you. You've forgotten that. We're not thinking clearly." She looked helpless and scared and she was shaking all over.

He knew how to prove he meant it. "Come here," he whispered, pulling her onto his lap.

"What are you doing?"

"I'm kissing you," he said and kept doing it until she released a shuddering exhale and softened against him.

He held her gaze, telling her to trust him, then reached under her skirt to stroke her. She was easy to reach because she wore no underwear.

"It's not even dark," she breathed, shuddering at his touch, growing wetter with each brush of his finger, her eyes shining at him. "Anyone could see."

"I told you I don't care." He kissed her neck, his fingers sliding along her swollen sex. "I want us to fly together."

"Mike." Fire lit her eyes. He loved that he could get that reaction from her. She hung on to him, giving in, kissing him with an open mouth, her body trembling. He felt every vibration under his own skin, as though they were one body.

He felt dizzy with the movement of the Ferris wheel and his desire for her. He knew it was crazy that he didn't care if anyone saw them, but for now all he wanted was to be inside her, giving her pleasure, taking his own.

He undid his zipper and shifted so he could enter

her. He held her hips as the car made its slow circle, and thrust with care, minimizing the car's rocking.

"We *are* flying," she said, riding him and the Ferris wheel.

He wished they were naked in the summer dusk. He wanted to see her brave, bare body silhouetted against the sunset sky.

Please stay.

The words formed in his mind, as true as his need to breathe. This wasn't about wanting an endless vacation or an escape from duty. This was about the two of them together, what they meant to each other, the way she opened his eyes. The way he hoped to help her see her own possibilities, overcome her doubts.

Autumn kissed him, then pressed herself close, almost as if she was avoiding the emotion in his face.

He felt her tighten around his cock. She was about to come. He was close, too. As soon as she made the sound that signaled her release, he joined her, holding her as they lunged through the pleasure, making sure she wouldn't fall.

He felt her heart banging against his own. She tucked her head under his chin, dissolving against him. He kissed her hair, breathed her in as they rose and fell slowly against the summer sky, the basket swaying. The mesquite leaves looked like black lace against the glowing sky. Mourning doves called to them.

The feeling grew stronger. *Stay here, Autumn.*

Or, hell, take me with you.

All he knew was that this couldn't end. He looked down at her in his arms. She was so beautiful. Her hair had pulled free of the knot she'd tied it in and it brushed her shoulders and his shirt. She looked wild and free, a sweet sprite whose job was to show him how to live.

"I don't want this to be over, Autumn," he said.

She pulled back, startled. "It has to be. For lots of reasons."

"But we're good for each other. We can help each other."

"We've already done that. You've already given me more confidence. And I've helped you take it easier."

"We can be more to each other."

"It's enough." She looked tortured. "Don't ruin the time we have left. We could never survive ordinary living. We have separate lives. Don't you see that? That's why this is so great."

He opened his mouth to argue with her, but the car reached the ground. "We should get back to town," she said and pushed herself up and out of the car.

He watched her at the control box, so determined, so sure as he circled up and away from her. When the car reached the ground, she put on the brakes and when he jumped out it seemed as though his heart hit the dirt before his feet did.

13

STANDING THERE, WAITING FOR MIKE to get off the Ferris wheel, Autumn could hardly breathe. His face was so sad and disappointed. Her heart felt like a fist in her chest.

He came close and forced a smile. "Let's go to your place," he said, clearly trying again to pretend things were normal.

"Sure," she said, wishing they could be. Why did he have to ruin everything? Sure, they cared about each other. And, yes, it was more than sex. But they couldn't throw their lives into chaos over it. They had no business falling in love.

As she pulled into the driveway a little while later—Mike was hidden in her backseat—she saw Barbara standing on the porch with yet another bowl of salsa. Convincing the woman to enter the contest might have been a judgment error. Barbara obsessed over every dash of salt or pinch of cilantro.

Autumn parked in the garage, let Mike into the house, then met Barbara on the porch.

"Here." Barbara thrust a salsa-loaded chip at her mouth. At least this would be quick, since Autumn's gruff neighbor wasn't much on the niceties.

Autumn savored the bite. "Mmm. Tangy, rich, nicely seasoned. But I liked the last two better."

"I agree, but which one is best?"

"I liked the one before this one—it had a nice blend of onion and garlic."

Barbara looked past her, as if asking to be invited in. Shoot. Not a good time. "I'd ask you in, but I've got a killer headache," she said, which wasn't even a lie.

"I'll make you some aloe vera and peppermint gel caps."

"I'll be fine."

"I have to make 'em anyway. In the morning." She thrust the salsa at her. "Enjoy." Then she marched away.

"Thanks a lot," she called. Barbara waved a hand without turning.

A honk made Autumn look up. Mr. Scranton waved at her before he pulled into his garage.

"How's that car running?" Eric Sands called to her from his open garage across the street, where he had his truck hood up, a mesh-covered light making his garage glow white.

"Working great! Thanks." He'd fixed Jasmine's idle.

Autumn carried the salsa into the kitchen, the cats trailing her, and found Mike studying the terrarium.

"Pretty fancy habitat," he said, glancing at her.

"I know. All that love and attention wasted on cold-blooded creatures."

"You think love can be wasted?"

"If it's not returned, yes."

"Maybe the mere act of loving is enough."

"I don't know." Her own emotions were too confused to figure that out. She noticed the chuckwalla hadn't touched its kale, usually his favorite green. "Why aren't you eating, Chuck?"

"You named him?" Mike asked.

"Had to. *Chuckwalla* is a mouthful."

"Look, he's saying hello to you."

The lizard did a few push-ups, head tilted her way.

"He always does that." But she couldn't help smiling at the thought that he recognized her.

"You like these guys. Admit it."

"They're fun to watch." She liked their hardiness, how the desert extremes didn't faze them one bit. She liked their wrinkles, their little claws, the flicking lids, the mouths that seemed to smile. She liked Mike standing here admiring them with her. What the hell was happening to her?

Mike put his arms around her, held her close and kissed her neck through her hair. "I have an idea," he murmured, making her tremble.

"You do?" Thank God. He meant something sexy. He was getting them back on track. She was grateful and relieved.

"Why don't you do one of those lap dances for me?"

She turned to him, smiling. "Really?"

"Yeah. I'd like that a lot."

"What a good idea," she said, especially because it was a reminder of how different their lives were. "Come on, then." She led him into the living room and pushed him into a chair. "I'll give you the full treatment."

"Can't wait."

She decided sex-in-the-office was the perfect routine. Fingers shaking, she covered her bikini top, thong and black stockings with a white silk blouse, buttons mostly open, one of Mike's neckties tied loosely and her choco-late blazer, unbuttoned. She taped her skirt up into a miniskirt and tied her hair up with a ribbon, then grabbed a notepad and pen from her nightstand.

In the living room, she flicked on an R&B track and strutted to him, snapping her hips side to side like gunshots. "I'll need your signature, Mayor Mike," she said breathily, bending low, swaying her hips, holding out the notepad and pen.

He scribbled a signature, staring at her chest.

"It's so warm, don't you think?" she said, dancing a little as she slid out of her jacket, pleased at the hot gleam in his eyes as he watched her every move.

"We should relax, don't you think? It's casual Friday." She undid her tie and tossed it at him. He didn't move to catch it, just watched her as she undid the last two buttons of her blouse, then let it slide from her arms. She ran her hands across her breasts through her bikini top, took a slow turn, then, with a quick move, freed her breasts from the small triangles.

Mike groaned and reached for her hips.

"Eh-eh-eh," she said, backing away slightly. "I do all the touching." She braced herself on the chair arms and slid her breasts across his shirt, giving a fake moan.

But that felt strange. Empty. She glanced at Mike, but that was worse because she saw how he felt. She forced her game face into place, pulled herself back, desperate to do this right, but suddenly not sure at all anymore.

Mike caught her hands. "Hey. Where'd you go?"

"I'm right here." She tried to smile.

"No, you're not. Don't disappear on me, Autumn."

"I'm not…I'm…" But he was right. She hid behind this sexy smile.

"Be with me." He pulled her onto his lap.

She tried to hold back, to keep her distance so she could dance, but his arms felt so good around her she just curled into his lap.

He looked at her with those espresso eyes and there was lust in them and so much more.

"I love you, Autumn." He spoke the words clearly and seriously and straight out, not fleeting, groaned in climax. He meant it.

"You make me feel more alive," he continued. "When I'm with you I want to do things—things I've always wanted to do and new things. Start a flight school, learn to hang glide, hell, sing karaoke on open mike night at Louie's."

"Try not to sound crazy," she said, wanting suddenly for this to be real. "You'll ruin it."

"And you love me, too?"

"I care about you. I don't know." She was afraid to even think it.

"You do. You love me." He laughed and stood, lifting her into his arms. "Come and show me."

He carried her into the bedroom in his arms. It was silly and romantic and she should laugh, but she couldn't. She just held on to his neck and let him lower her to the narrow bed, pull off her costume and undress himself in the dim light of the room. It seemed like a feverish dream.

He kissed her mouth, her breasts and touched her everywhere, his fingers moving with such tenderness she felt aroused and taken care of in equal measure.

He entered her as easily as thought, and his slow strokes built her pleasure with steady assurance. Each thrust repeated his message to her, *I love you... You're mine... We belong together.*

She opened to him, let him deep into her body and her heart. The closer her climax came, the more she felt the pressure of tears in her eyes. They were making love now and there was no going back to just sex. It was wonderful and scary and Autumn didn't know how this would end.

Her orgasm shuddered through her, making her boneless with pleasure. She felt Mike's release and, when it was over, he pulled her close to him in the Huffmans' squeaky guest bed and twined his legs with hers, as if to prevent her escape.

But she wasn't going anywhere. "Now what do we do?" she asked softly.

"We'll figure it out."

"I have school and the revue. I have commitments."

"You have to quit dancing some time, right?"

"Stripping, Mike. It's stripping. That's what I do. I promised Nevada and Jasmine two years at least. Plus, the money is great and I need to save for my business. I'm not ashamed—"

"Okay. I get it." She'd been defensive, she realized. He stroked her softly. "We don't have to decide anything now."

"*You* could move. Why not? Come to Phoenix with Mark." She paused. "No, you can't."

"We'll figure it out," he said again.

How could he sound so sure? She had no idea what the solution would be. She wasn't positive they weren't dreaming.

"How did you start?" he asked after a while. "Dancing—I mean stripping."

"Why do you ask?" She rose on an elbow and looked down at him, prepared to see judgment in his face, but all she saw was open interest.

"It's a big part of your life. I want to know how it happened."

"Okay." She looked across the room. "I needed money. A lot of money. My baby brother owed a guy a thousand bucks, plus his car was about to be repossessed and I knew he'd never get it together to ride the bus to his job and it would be downhill from there."

Mike rubbed her arm as if to soothe her.

"A friend had bragged about the money she made at this strip club. It was amateur night and I thought, what the hell?"

"You were helping your family."

"Don't try to make me sound noble. I made a thousand bucks in two nights. It was easy so I stuck with it. That's me, Mike. Easy road all the way."

"You had a rough childhood, Autumn. It's remarkable that you rose above all that."

"Says the orphan at sixteen. The point is that's how we are—my brothers and me. They're always in need of cash for bail over stupid shit. They're barely making it in life and they blame the world."

"You're not like that."

"I'm not that different." She was confessing her deepest doubts to Mike. He'd always seemed to see through her and now that he loved her she felt open to him.

"I kept telling myself I'd save up for college, but then I figured I'd missed my chance, and the girls counted on me at Moons and Duke counted on me and the months turned into years and the years went by."

"But you're in school now. Look how far you've come." He held her gaze, squeezed her arm. "Really. Let it sink in."

"I guess so. I'm doing good in school."

"There you go."

"So far."

"And you nailed this internship. Hell, you're practically my deputy mayor."

She laughed, letting the satisfaction wash over her. Before she knew it she'd climbed right onto Jasmine's pink cloud. "How can this ever work?" she asked, desperately wanting it to.

"Love makes all things possible," Mike whispered.

She didn't even laugh.

THE NEXT DAY, Autumn was relieved when Mike went with Mark to show the Desert Paradise to Wayne Whittaker. Since they'd confessed their love, she felt nervous around him.

She was behaving oddly herself. She'd actually called the U of A's business department to ask about transfer requirements, her heart in her throat the entire time. She was going over the festival checklist when the door jangled.

She'd forgotten Evelyn was running errands, so she was surprised when a female voice said, "Hello."

She immediately recognized her as Lydia. Even if she hadn't seen photos, the Day-Glo green knitted sling in which the woman held her baby had to be Evelyn's handiwork. "You're Lydia." She stood and extended a hand. "I'm so glad to meet you."

"Sorry I didn't call, but I was out shopping and just stopped in. How are you doing?"

"Pretty well, I think."

Lydia looked around. "Looks like you've settled in."

Autumn followed her gaze. Autumn's bowling shirt hung on the door hook, the bucket of golf balls rested against the back wall. She'd brought in her own boom box and pinned motivational quotes to the wall. "I hope it doesn't look like I'm taking over."

"No, no. It's great. You're on the team?" Lydia picked up the framed photo of the bowling team Autumn had put on her desk.

"Yeah. I'm having fun."

"I was surprised that Mike had signed up a team. It's not like him to recreate."

She only smiled, thinking of all the recreating they'd done over the last three weeks.

"So what are you working on?" She moved to look over Autumn's shoulder.

Autumn showed her the research on group purchasing of computer equipment she'd done for the police department and the used fire trucks she'd located for a good price.

"Wow. You make me look bad," Lydia said. "I never had time to do much research."

"I just wanted to do a good job. I didn't intend to—"

"No, no. It's great. It's a relief, really, to know things are under control here. This little guy has turned my world upside down." She looked down at the sleeping baby, cheek pressed against Lydia's breast. It was so intimate, so adoring that Autumn felt a tug inside. She'd never thought of herself as maternal, but this warm longing had to mean something.

Lydia sighed, then looked at Autumn. "The truth is, I'd like to extend my leave. If my husband stays busy— he's in construction, which is always iffy—we could swing it. Would you consider working longer?"

"I have school," she said, "and a job." The idea made it hard to breathe. Here was a solution, at least short-term. She could stay on in Lydia's place.

But Jasmine and Nevada would be devastated if she left the revue. Something stabbed at her about that, a lost feeling. If she stopped stripping, what could she count on?

"It was just a thought. Maybe I'll get bored. I mean, soon enough he'll be flushing action-figures down the toilet and using a Sharpie on my Laura Ashley wallpaper, right? Right now I'm so happy I feel stunned, but things always change."

This was true. Feelings changed, too. There was a lesson in here if Autumn could get down off her pink cloud and learn it.

The baby opened his eyes and seemed to recognize his mother for a happy second, then he grunted and went red in the face.

"Is he all right?" Autumn asked, worried.

A terrible stench filled the air.

"Now he is. Gotta change him. How he creates these poisonous dumps from my sweet milk, I'll never know. Excuse me, would you?" She headed to the bathroom.

Autumn was at the printer when Mike came in.

He was at her side in a few quick strides. "God, I missed you." He pulled her into his arms.

"Mike, Lydia's in the—"

He kissed her and she broke away as fast as she could, but not before Lydia emerged from the bathroom and caught sight of them.

"Lydia, hi!" Mike went as red as the baby had been.

Lydia seemed shocked, but she pretended not to notice. "I just stopped by to meet Autumn and see how things are going…."

"She's doing great," he said and his eyes lingered on her.

The door clanged again. It was Evelyn this time, and the distraction was a blessed relief. "What's happening?" Evelyn asked, squeezing into the alcove with them. "Lydia, good to see you." She focused on the baby. "Isn't that the most precious thing?" She fingered the sling, not the baby.

"I love it, Evelyn," Lydia said. "And the booties and the hat and the blanket and the door hanger and the mobile and…everything."

"I'm so glad." Evelyn beamed, then looked at Mike. "So have you held him, Mike?"

"No, I—"

"He's freshly changed," Lydia said, extracting the baby from the carrier and extending him to Mike.

"I'm not very… I've never actually—"

"He won't melt or crumble," Lydia said, laughing. "Just hold him against your body."

Mike did as she'd said and looked down at the infant in wonder. "He's so small, but all there."

Autumn's heart clutched with tenderness. What a great father Mike would make. Could she ever be a mother? She'd never even thought of herself as a wife, let alone a parent. She was thirty-five years old, anyway. Too old, right?

Love makes all things possible. She got a funny, fuzzy hope that it could be true.

"Now if that doesn't give you two ideas, I don't know what will," Evelyn said. She looked from Mike to Autumn.

Autumn felt her jaw drop.

"Give us ideas?" Mike said.

"That's how it works—you date, you get married, you have kids." She ticked off the words on her fingers. "Sometimes the order varies, but that's generally the routine."

"Evelyn," Mike said, "I don't—"

"We don't—" Autumn said at the same time.

"Come on. I'm not blind. You're all the time picking on her, popping in and out of each other's offices all day long. I'm about to knit you a little Do Not Disturb sign for the bowling alley restroom."

"I didn't realize we were so obvious," Mike said.

Autumn's face burned with heat.

"No one's started a pool yet on when you're going to pop the question or anything—"

"A pool?" Mike went white.

"Just kidding. I don't think anyone else knows."

"I knew you weren't gay," Lydia said, beaming. She leaned over to kiss him on the cheek. "I kept telling people."

"People think I'm gay?"

"It's because you go to the opera," Autumn explained.

"And we'll keep it on the down-low, won't we, Lydia?" Evelyn pretended to zip her lip. "Until you two settle in."

"Oh, absolutely. I'm happy for you both," Lydia said.

"We don't know what we're doing," Autumn said, glancing at Mike, who looked at her as if he never wanted to take his eyes off her.

"We're working it out," Mike said, holding her gaze.

"We know that." Evelyn sighed. "In the meantime, I went ahead and signed for the PA system, Mike. And I took care of the silent auction pick-ups, too. You forgot."

"Sorry. I've been—"

"Busy. Yeah. We got that."

Lydia left, Evelyn got busy and Mike followed Autumn into her office. Shutting the door, he kissed her.

"Maybe we shouldn't do this here," she said.

"Why not? Evelyn's probably already knitting you a wedding dress."

"Stop." She put a finger to his lips and stepped away from him. "We don't even live in the same place."

"Not yet." He shrugged and she couldn't believe how ready she was to believe that they would just magically work everything out. "What's this?" He took the printout from her fingers.

She explained the screaming deal on the fire trucks she'd found.

"Good job. Why don't you find us a grant with funds for an administrator and you're hired? It's not straight accounting, but there would be plenty of numbers."

"You're dreaming, Mike." He was in a pink limbo, too. "How did it go with Whittaker and the Desert Paradise?"

"Pretty well. He's going to run the numbers by his business manager and his accountant."

"So he's interested?"

"Don't get your hopes up. These things fall through all the time."

And the two of them might fall through, too, she reminded herself.

"Before I forget," Mike said, "Mark insists I approve some changes in the pageant. I put it off as long as I can. Come with me, okay? Tomorrow night?"

"Sure." Pageant changes…she vaguely remembered Jasmine talking about the pageant that night of prickly pear margaritas.

"So…you want kids, don't you?" Mike asked.

"Mike, what are you talking about?"

"Just holding that baby was…nice. I know. I'm getting ahead of myself. It's just that this is…"

"Like a dream."

"Yeah. I guess."

She pinched his arm.

"Ouch."

"You felt that?"

He pinched her gently back. "You?"

"Yep."

"Looks like we're both awake." He grinned like a goof.

"Or dreaming we pinched each other." Doubt nibbled at her heart the way the angelfish attacked the flakes on the surface of their tank.

"Then I hope we never wake up." Mike pulled her into his arms and when he kissed her, she felt like Sleeping Beauty in reverse. Her Prince Charming was kissing her to sleep.

14

AUTUMN ARRIVED AT THE pageant rehearsal early at Jasmine's request—she wanted a favor—and found her friend dressed like a dance hall girl in a black lace corset, feathered hat, fishnets, short boots and a knee-length ruffled skirt thick with petticoats. She was adjusting a similar costume—except in red—on the director, Sheila. What the hell was going on?

"Hello," she said, making both women turn.

"Autumn! Perfect timing. I need a third dancer. Will you do it?"

"A third dancer?"

"Yes. You'd be a soiled dove in Arizona Rose's Desert Palace."

"You put the whorehouse in the pageant?"

"Isn't it exciting?" Sheila said. "Three new scenes, a dance number and two songs. I wrote the songs and scenes and Jasmine did the dance numbers."

"Nevada did the choreography," Jasmine said. "She e-mailed me a simple routine. And I play Arizona Rose."

"She's perfect, too. And don't you love this costume?" Sheila said, doing a slow turn. "I've gotta touch base with the orchestra." She hurried off and Jasmine turned to her.

"So, it's a simple can-can with a little chair work and

some splits. I've got a costume roughed out for you. Will you do it?"

"I suppose I could," she said. "And you changed the whole thing so it focuses on the hookers?"

"Soiled doves. And that's the true history. Copper Corners was founded on love."

"Sex for money is not love, Jasmine."

"It was different back then. The Desert Palace was like the community center. Anyway, this pageant is much livelier than the stodgy old version. And it feels right for me to play Arizona Rose opposite the man I love, don't you think?"

"I guess." Somehow, Jasmine's delight made it seem all right.

"So, stay for practice after this, okay? Assuming Mike approves it. Mark's a little worried, since he can be kind of uptight."

"Don't underestimate the man," she said with a smile that had to look, hell, wistful. "He's more broad-minded than you might think." He'd fallen in love with a stripper, after all.

Jasmine stared at her. "Are you okay?"

"I'm fine. I don't know. I'm just…"

"Happy? You look happy."

"I guess so. Are you happy, Jas? With Mark, I mean?"

"Uh, yeah." Jasmine looked at her as if she'd lost her mind, then touched her forehead with the back of her hand. "No fever. What's wrong with you? Why aren't you telling me to slow down and guard my heart?"

The door at the back of the auditorium creaked open and Autumn turned to see Mike silhouetted by the rectangle of star-lit desert sky, just like that first night.

This time he galloped down the burgundy-carpeted aisle straight for her. She waited, her heart in her throat, her body dying to press against his, to make contact, to—

"Oh. My. God. You and Mike?"

"Huh?" She turned to her friend.

"I don't believe it. When did you…? How did you…? Oh, I'm so happy for you!" Jasmine threw her arms around Autumn, and this time when Autumn bit her tongue, it tasted sweet.

She hadn't meant to tell anyone yet and they'd sworn Evelyn and Lydia to secrecy, but Jasmine had guessed, so what the hell? "We don't know how this will work or what we'll do, but—"

"Love makes—"

"All things possible. Yeah. I hope you're right."

WHEN HE SAW Autumn standing in the auditorium, Mike couldn't take his eyes off her. He wanted to drag her into his arms and kiss her in front of God, the pageant cast, hell, the whole town.

As he'd held Lydia's baby he'd been swamped with the desire to have one of his own. With Autumn. A baby created by their love.

He had to get moving on this fast, get Autumn into his house, get her a job, set her up at the U of A, settle her in before she scared herself and looked down at the thin wire they were inching across.

It was all too new and so tentative. And he wanted it to be solid and sure. Autumn was clinging to being a stripper in self defense. She was done with all that. What she needed was a fresh start in a safe place and he was determined to give it to her.

As he headed down the aisle toward Autumn, her friend Jasmine threw her arms around her and hugged her hard. For some reason, the woman was dressed like a saloon girl.

"What's up?" he asked when he was close enough.

"The new pageant is great, Mike," Autumn said, her eyes gleaming. "It's about the power of love."

"Oh, yeah?" he said, not really caring at the moment.

She grabbed his hand and leaned close. "Jasmine guessed," she whispered.

"Are you okay with that?"

"I think so."

"Then I am, too." This was a good sign coming from her.

"Mark will be so happy for you," Jasmine said. As if on cue, Mark called to him from the stage. "You're here. Let's do this then." He was dressed in his role of miner Josiah Bremmer with dusty clothes, a battered felt hat and a pickax.

"Do I look like a madam to you?" Jasmine asked Mike.

"A madam? I guess. Sure."

Happy, she turned and ran up to the stage.

"What's a madam doing in the founder's pageant?" he asked Autumn, starting to feel uneasy. And the new pageant was all about the power of love?

"Places!" Sheila shouted.

"You'll see. Let's sit." Autumn led the way past the rows where a few cast members watched and they sat in the front row. He just wanted to be alone with her again. Luckily, this shouldn't take long since the cast would only perform the changed scenes.

Sheila stepped in front of the curtain, thanked them for coming and cued the musicians, who played some of the overture before the curtain opened to reveal Mark and Jasmine standing in front of a set painted to look like the entrance to the Copper Strike Mine.

"You have my heart, Josiah Bremmer," Jasmine said, "so I cannot return to Illinois. Chicago Rose is dead, born again as Arizona Rose. I will open a new establishment right here. It will be a palace in the desert, a place of pleasure and a symbol of our love."

"I love you, my Arizona Rose." Mark threw down his hat and pulled Jasmine into his arms for a kiss that went on far too long. The curtains closed and Mike turned to Autumn. "Is she saying what I think she's saying?"

"Yep. Copper Corners grew up around a cathouse, not the mine. I found it in an online history."

"You're joking."

"No. I think it's cool. Isn't love a better reason to start a town than gold fever and greed?"

He didn't answer, but he knew now why Mark had insisted he see the changes. This would rock Copper Corners.

The curtains opened onto a set painted like a saloon, and Sheila sang about miners needing company for the lonely nights, after which she and Jasmine did a dance that involved chest shimmies, high kicks and some sultry moves with a chair.

The curtains closed and everyone clapped and Autumn squeezed his arm. "Jasmine asked me to dance, too. Isn't that great?"

For God's sake. The founder's pageant was for families. This was all wrong. The town expected the familiar tale of the Copper Strike Mine and the

Common Bread Colony. He pictured Josiah Bremmer's great-great-great grandchildren, who sat in the seats of honor, front row, wearing corsages and boutonnieres.

This was the damned 150th anniversary. They'd spent money on costume designs, more props and sets. He wasn't about to embarrass anyone.

"This won't work," he muttered to her.

"What do you mean?" She turned startled eyes to him.

Sheila pushed through the curtains. "So, what do you think, Mayor?" she asked breathlessly. "Isn't this wonderful?"

"I'll come backstage," he said, pushing to his feet. He felt Autumn staring at him, mouth open. Then she followed him.

He had to straighten this out diplomatically. Sheila stood with Mark and Jasmine waiting for him in the middle of stage. The cast had followed him and Autumn backstage, too.

"Could we speak privately?" he asked Sheila.

"Why?"

He might as well just say it. "Look, I know you all worked hard on this," he said, turning to include the group, "but you'll need to go back to the old pageant."

"The old pageant?" Sheila said.

"Even if it's true about the bordello, there will be families in the audience and that dance is too suggestive for children."

"But it's meant to be…evocative," Sheila said.

"It's flat-out vulgar," he said bluntly.

"So maybe skip the chair part?" Mark said.

"Mark!" Jasmine sounded stung. "You said you loved the dance."

"I do, but it *is* a family event," Mark mumbled.

"We'll be better off with the old script," Mike said. "I won't ask people to celebrate the fact their town was built on prostitution—and I'm not even convinced that's true."

"But the story is about the sacrifices we make for love," Sheila said. "Arizona Rose gave up fame and success for the lawless Arizona Territory to be with the man she loved."

"The pageant is supposed to make us feel proud, not embarrass us."

"It's the truth," Autumn snapped. Everyone turned to her. "Face it, Mike. If it weren't for a houseful of hookers, you wouldn't have a town to run."

"You're overstating the case," he said, surprised at how angry she was.

"And you're being an ass." Her eyes blazed at him. She turned to Jasmine. "I'd be honored to dance with you. Just let me know what you decide." She gave him a last glare and strode off.

He got the message. *You're a small-town hick with a small mind.* She'd taken a simple matter of public sensibilities and turned it into a moral judgment on his part that somehow included her. Lord.

"We worked so hard," Jasmine said with dismay.

"I know and I'm sorry. I should have been at an earlier rehearsal. I apologize for that."

"We'll figure out a compromise, right, Mike?" Mark put his arm around Jasmine, but she shrugged it off.

"We'll talk," Mike said, "but I can't promise anything."

His mind was on Autumn, on something he'd seen in her face when she left. Relief. She'd been relieved to be angry at him. What the hell was that about?

AUTUMN FELT THE WAY SHE HAD the time she fell backward from the pole and got the wind knocked out of her. Listening to Mike defend Copper Corners's honor, as if a few high kicks were too vulgar for decent people, she saw him clearly for the first time.

You might be able to take the mayor out of the small town, but you couldn't take the small town out of the mayor. Besides, he'd never leave. He belonged in Copper Corners and she belonged miles and miles away from here.

Stripping was not a respectable career or legitimate entertainment to Mike and never would be.

At least she'd learned it now, before she did something stupid like transfer to the U of A, take a job with Mike and then find out he was ashamed of her.

They'd both been dreaming.

Shaking with fury and hurt, she got into her car, her vision blurry with unshed tears. She was so frustrated, so angry. She had to *do* something. Passing the hardware store, she knew exactly what. She ran in and bought three boxes of golf balls, then headed out to the Desert Paradise. Luckily, her club was still in the trunk.

Mike had made her feel as small as she had in high school. She would not let anyone do that to her ever again. She was a grown woman who could bring men to their knees with her moves—not some meek, small-town girl ashamed of her sexual power.

Love makes all things possible. Bullshit. Love made you forget what you knew cold. People didn't change. Mike was a small-town guy with the hots for a stripper. Behind closed doors he was okay with sexy stuff, but out in public, in front of respectable citizens, oh, no, too offensive.

She roared into the resort parking lot, spun gravel as she jerked into a space and jammed on her brakes. In a couple of minutes she'd laid out the first box of balls in a long row at the tee line.

The Ferris wheel rose against the starlit sky to her left and she could pick out the darker shapes of the not-yet-assembled rides here and there on the course. She'd aim to hit them, just for fun.

She took a few practice swings, loving the way the club grip felt in her fingers, loving the power in her arms.

She went at the balls as though her life depended on hitting them for miles. One, two, three, four, five, six balls without stopping.

She paused to catch her breath and rub the sweat from her palms, the tears from her cheeks.

So maybe she'd overreacted about Mike's response to the pageant. Maybe the dance had been too racy for kids. He had a point there. But the true problem was still there. She and Mike were from different worlds. They could never build a life together.

She set up the other twelve balls from her first box, pleased to hear the last one ping against one of the rides. At least she was getting better at golf.

She laid out the next box, six at a time, and by the time she'd finished with them, she was sweaty and aching and almost finished crying.

She'd set up balls from the third box when she heard the crunch of gravel and turned to see familiar head-lights pulling in.

Mike. Her heart froze in her chest. She was happy to see him—she couldn't help that—but she dreaded it, too. They might as well get it over with, she guessed. She waited, breathing hard, trying to ignore the waging battle her emotions were carrying on inside her. She'd gotten too attached, she was too dependent on Mike. She'd forgotten who she was and what she wanted.

"When you weren't home, I figured you'd be here," he said, stopping at the far end of the tee line.

Her heart ached at the sight of him silhouetted against the sky, troubled, but still loving her. She could see it in his eyes, even at this distance.

So what? She had to be strong. She'd finally woken up from the dream they were in. "So, did you shut them down?"

"We're talking. We'll see."

"They had a big, sexy story to tell the town, but you're too much of a tight ass to let them tell it."

"It's a founder's day pageant, not an exposé. I'm responsible for it. I won't put on something that shocks people."

"You're not the town daddy, Mike. These people watch TV. They understand entertainment. They'd probably love it. And if not, maybe it would wake them up a little, make them admit they're human." She whacked a ball hard.

The dance could be less bold, of course. The revue had less nudity than a regular strip act in order to appeal to a broader audience. Still. Her point was valid. She glared at Mike, her hands still vibrating from her swing.

"You're making this about us," Mike said levelly.

"It *is* about us. You hate that I'm a stripper. Admit it."

Something flickered in his gaze. "Okay. Yes. I hate the idea of men eating you up with their eyes. No man who loved you would feel differently. That doesn't make me a tight ass. That makes me human."

"I'm proud of what I do. I like that I can make men want me. I like that you want me."

"So, that's it. To you I'm just another joker thinking with his equipment?"

"You pretend to be better than other men. You're not. You're just as horny and hot-blooded as any man I strip for." The words hurt to say.

"Was that the point all along? You want me on my knees, at your beck and call? You crook your finger and I come." He sounded angry now, as though he'd been used, which wasn't fair.

"You never complained before."

"You're the pretender, Autumn. You don't want to be a stripper anymore. You're beyond that. You're in school."

"I'm not ashamed of what I've done or who I am."

"Oh, yeah? Then why didn't you tell me you were a stripper when you applied for the job? If you're so proud of it, why keep it a secret?"

"Because you would have seen me differently, like all men do. You wouldn't care that I was smart and skilled and resourceful and— Oh, forget it!" She broke down, stung by his accusation, afraid he was right and angry he'd said it.

He strode to her, reaching out. "I don't want to hurt you. I'm sorry. Let's stop this."

"You're right." She pulled away, lifted her chin. "We do have to stop. We have to stop fooling ourselves." She stared up at the desert sky, then out to where she'd been hitting balls and finally at him. "The vacation is over, Mike. I could never live in this choked little town. And I could never be with a man who's ashamed of me."

"I'm not the one who's ashamed, Autumn. When you danced for me, you disappeared. Your eyes were blank. You don't love stripping. At least not anymore."

"Bullshit!" She wanted to slap him.

"I can see I can't win. If I'm proud of you for moving on in your life, it's because I'm ashamed of what you were. If I disagree with you, it's because I think I'm better than you. No matter what I say, I'll be wrong."

He was so full of anguish, she couldn't be angry at him anymore. And, besides, he was correct. "You're right. You can't win. Neither can I. Wanting to be together isn't enough."

"Why not? We can make it work."

"We're too different. You're ready to move to Phoenix? To stand around with Mark and pass out flyers to promote the revue? Because that's what he'll be doing for Jasmine, I guarantee."

"You're exaggerating."

"Not a bit. Jasmine loves the act and if Mark loves her, he's stuck with it."

"Forget about Mark and Jasmine. What about us?"

"What about us? You belong in Copper Corners and I don't. I don't fit here."

"You fit with me. You could fit here if you wanted to. Small towns can be insular and maybe the people gossip too much. That's human nature. But we also care about each other. We face the people we've wronged or confused or hurt and we make it right. We don't run away."

"You think I'm running away? I'm facing how impossible this is."

"I love you, Autumn, and I'm willing to try to make this work. But you have to want it, too."

"And I don't," she said bluntly. "This was wrong from the beginning. Maybe that's the problem. I used the fact you were hot for me to get you to hire me."

"That's not true."

"I seduced you. That's what happened." The sarcasm that usually made her feel strong seemed as bitter on her tongue as lemon in hot chocolate.

"Okay. I can play that game. I sexually harassed you—used my power as your boss to force you into my bed." His eyes, usually a hot brown, were now murky and dull. "You know that wasn't what happened, Autumn. You know that."

"It was close enough. The point is we have to end this."

He watched her for a long time, his chest moving with ragged breaths, his mouth thin with tension, his eyes turbulent as a monsoon storm. The breeze hummed through the mesquite trees and ruffled his hair. Something splashed in the pond. The desert sky, so full of possibilities before, seemed cold and distant and endlessly sad.

"Maybe you're right," he said finally.

"I know I am," she said, tears filling her eyes again. She looked down at the balls remaining on the ground, an uneven dot-to-dot in the moonlight, but she didn't have the strength to hit a single one.

"Can I borrow that?" he asked, reaching for her club.

She nodded, memorizing the brush of his fingers when he took the club. She thought about all the balls they'd hit and never picked up.

She walked to her car, listening to the whisk and whack of his swings, one after another, counterpoint to the throb of her heart.

All the way home, she pounded the steering wheel and yelled into the car, fighting tears. She was so upset that she passed the Huffmans' house and had to turn back.

Inside, she fed the lizards and turtles and found herself telling them what had happened. The fish got a little lecture on the importance of honesty in relationships. And the cats…well, she just hugged them, dripping tears into their fur.

She made herself a pitcher of prickly pear margaritas, which made her think of Esmeralda. Esmie would lecture her like crazy. *You did it. You kicked your heart to the curb.* She wasn't ready for that conversation. No way. So she went out onto the back patio to drink herself numb.

"Huh." Barbara's greeting was little more than a grunt from across the fence. In a few seconds she spoke again. "Want chips and salsa to go with that?" Of all the times for her grumpy neighbor to feel friendly.

"No thanks," she said. "Can I pour you one though?"

"No. Tequila tastes the same going down as coming back up."

Autumn laughed and approached the wall.

"You already look like the morning after," Barbara said, dependably blunt.

Autumn didn't comment, just surveyed the woman's backyard, jam-packed with flowers and bushes and a vine-covered trellis drowning in white blooms. She noticed a tire swing and wooden climbing apparatus. "You have children?"

"Yep. Grown twins. Boy and a girl. They're twenty-five now. I spend holidays in Phoenix with them—split the time between 'em."

"They don't come here?"

"They don't much like small towns."

"I can understand that." She noticed a row of Popsicle-stick crosses at the edge of the patio. "What are those for?"

Barbara looked. "The kids were into hamsters in kindergarten. We had a funeral every time one croaked."

"That's sweet." The tiny pets had been tucked beneath those markers for twenty years. Autumn couldn't imagine that kind of permanence.

"You remind me of my daughter," Barbara said. "You're restless and intense like she is. Except you've got a chip on your shoulder."

Autumn looked at the woman. "I beg your pardon?"

"No shame in that. I've got one, too, my daughter says. Things that aren't right stick with me, you know? I can't let 'em go." She shrugged.

Autumn nodded. "I know exactly what you mean." She gulped the rest of her margarita. "I'm the same."

"Might be why my kids don't visit so much after their father died. My son says I don't give people a chance—benefit of the doubt, he always says."

That was what Esmeralda had warned her about, too. During the birthday fortune and when she'd called. "Maybe they don't deserve the benefit of the doubt." She marched back to the pitcher and poured a second drink, then marched back. "Hell, you give someone another chance and they'll just hurt you all over again. What's the good of that? I say stick to your guns. What's right is right. What's wrong is wrong."

"I'll tell you what that'll get you," Barbara said, an odd fire in her eyes. "Living alone in a big house waiting for the next holiday because you know your kids won't welcome an in-between visit." She looked away, studied the hamster graveyard, blinking fast.

Autumn wasn't sure what to say. She'd never seen Barbara emotional. She waited quietly until the woman turned back to her.

"The point is that things aren't always so clear—good or bad, black or white, off the bus or on it. Sometimes it's in between. I'll get you those gel caps if you mean to finish that pitcher."

"Thanks," Autumn called to Barbara's retreating back. It was nice to have someone worrying about her hangover. Coming from Barbara, she knew the sentiment was sincere.

Was she right? Were things not always clear-cut? The idea bothered her. Were things between her and Mike not quite so simple? Esmie would say, *Oh, yes. Absolutely. You're getting it.* And nod her head for emphasis.

Autumn thought about the tea leaves Esmie had read on their birthday. To Autumn, the smear at the bottom of her cup looked like chicken pox or acne, but Esmie had pored over the mess like it was the golden ticket to happiness.

Changes? she'd said. *Oh, yes. In the three Hs—head and hearth and heart and the heart will lead.*

Oh, yeah? Look where Autumn's heart had led her…into aching misery. She had a bone to pick with her psychic friend. She'd have been a whole lot better off if she had kicked her heart to the curb.

"Ah, Esmie." She lifted her margarita in a rueful toast to the sliver of a moon.

She was startled to see a star shoot across the sky. That was so Esmie that Autumn got chills and a funny tickle in her chest like things weren't quite as settled as she thought they were.

15

A HORRIBLE GRINDING NOISE woke Autumn early the next morning. She sat up and grabbed her head. The two cats meowed in complaint. They'd been asleep on either side of her, furry earmuffs purring like engines, off and on all night.

She hadn't finished the pitcher, but she had a hangover all the same—her mouth was dusty as the desert, her stomach queasy and her head throbbed. But her worst pain had nothing to do with tequila. Her heart felt shattered.

She took two more of the aloe gel caps Barbara had given her, then got gingerly out of bed to stop the roar coming from the kitchen, where Jasmine was grinding coffee beans.

"Stop the torture! I'll talk," she said, palms pressed to her temples.

Jasmine smiled. "I'm helping you. Caffeine shrinks the blood vessels, thereby reducing the headache. I saw the remnants of your little pity party." She nodded at the blender and the prickly pear juice mix. "Caffeine helps migraines, too."

"Aren't you the font of health knowledge?"

"Don't bother being a bitch to me. Make up with Mike."

"Can't do it."

Grrrrrind.

"Ooooh, stop that."

Jasmine poured the ground beans into the paper filter. "I know I felt better once I gave Mark a piece of my mind. He has to start standing up to his big brother. He folds every time Mike disagrees with him like he's twelve years old again."

"So you and Mark had a fight?" she asked.

"Yeah." She slapped the cone into place with a sigh.

"I'm so sorry." She stood, ready to go hug her friend. "Sometimes two people can't bridge their differences."

Jasmine turned, the pot of water in her hand. "We fought, Autumn. We didn't break up."

"You worked it out?" She sat back down.

"A fight is an opportunity to get closer."

"So, you're still together?" she said, her thoughts trickling through the aching mush her brain had become.

"Of course. We love each other. And you and Mike will work it out, too."

"It's not that simple for us." Fearing Jasmine might go for the grinder again, she added, "Let's just say I'm not burying any hamsters around here."

"What are you talking about?"

"It's a long story. We just got carried away." She'd been swept up in her success on the job, by the intensity of their hot affair and forgotten who she really was. The Copper-Corners Autumn was like an added-on rumpus room—new and nice, but not quite part of the whole house. Eventually the new Autumn and the old Autumn would all blend together, but not yet, and she couldn't pretend to be different than she was for Mike. Or for anyone.

A meow made her look down to see Mocha and Marmalade swirling at her feet. When they caught her eye, they both leaped onto her lap, their purrs so loud they made her head throb.

"Those cats sure love you," Jasmine said.

She smiled sadly at them. "Where's your dignity? I'm leaving. Don't you know not to give away your hearts?"

"You don't always have to fight for what you want, Autumn," Jasmine said. "A gift horse is still a gift, Trojan or not."

"What?" Her head hurt too much for mixed metaphors.

"Sometimes happiness just falls in your lap."

"Maybe for you. Not for me."

"That's because you expect the worst, Ms. Glass Half Empty. Look how long you fought the idea of going to school. *Oh, it's too much money. Oh, I can't do it. Oh, there are no jobs.*" Jasmine handed her a mug filled with the first drips of coffee.

"Thanks." Autumn took a careful sip.

"Trust your love for Mike. It's real."

"I'll think about it, Doctor Jasmine. When did you get so wise?"

"You just underestimate me, hon. Keep your shower cool. Better for your hangover."

"Thanks." Jasmine had suddenly become a source of relationship advice and hangover tips.

Either Autumn had never really seen her friend's wisdom or Jasmine had changed. Or Autumn had. Or both. Or, hell, Mercury had aligned with Venus and if she could read her coffee grounds, they'd spell out a global SOS.

Autumn was too confused and in too much pain to figure it out. Right now, she had a lot of work to do, including the final meeting of the Founder's Day festival planning committee this very morning. The festival was in four days. She would do all she could to make sure it came off without a hitch. For the town and for Mike.

Mike. Tears swelled every time she thought of him. She loved him. How else could she feel so much pain? She missed him so much. She missed how his eyes bored into her, the way his arms around her made her feel as if everything would be fine, even when it wouldn't. But that was over. She had to push past her sadness, do her best to finish the job and move into the future she'd mapped out for herself. She was not quitting. That was one good way she'd changed. Mike was right about that.

MIKE WOKE TO THE SOUND of beer bottles crashing beside his skull.

"What the hell happened here?" his brother asked.

He looked up from where he lay in the den in front of the TV, surrounded by the empty Tecates that had soothed him last night but left their boot prints on his brain this morning.

Mark tapped another bottle, which clinked into its mate. "You have a party last night? All by yourself?"

"Yeah." Mike sat up, then grabbed his head. Drowning his sorrows had been foolish, but what else was new? He'd been a fool from the minute he shook hands with Autumn Beshkin in her business suit and killer underwear.

"I'm the one who should have gotten drunk," Mark said, dropping onto the sofa with a leathery squeak. "I don't have the balls God gave me."

"What are you talking about?"

"You've got to loosen up about the pageant, Mike."

"Loosen up? I am responsible for it, for the families who come to see it, for the money we spent, for—"

"You're responsible for way too much. Let the town go, Mike. Hell, let me go."

Anger shot through Mike. He'd had enough of the people he loved criticizing him. "Look, I do what needs to be done."

"You do too much," Mark snapped back. "For me and the town."

"I'm not stopping you from a damn thing."

"You're right. I've been weak. Because I made mistakes in the past, I doubted myself and let you tell me what to do."

Mike stared at his brother, listening hard. "Where did all this come from?"

"Jasmine got mad at me because I folded when you objected to the new pageant. She pointed out that I'm not thirteen, sneaking into the living room at midnight to play *Donkey Kong,* hoping you won't catch me. I'm also not the same guy who fell for Brenda's line of bull. After a while, I got her point. I'm a grown-up and I need to act like it. Stand up to you, hold my own opinions."

"I never intended to undermine you," he said softly.

"I know you want the best for me. But it's my life, mistakes and all. You don't have to pick up the pieces when I screw up. It's my life and my clean-up duty."

"I get it." He shook his head, caught short by Mark's words. Maybe he'd gone overboard with him, treated him as though he was still twelve. "What can I do to make it up to you?"

"Maybe take a little advice from me for a change."

"Sounds fair." He managed a smile.

"First, let the new pageant happen. They'll tone down the dance. It *was* R-rated. I'll give you the history to read. You can see for yourself the story's not just about a cathouse. Arizona Rose was a civilizing force in the town. In a way, it's a story of women's rights, the way women worked behind the scenes to bring order to the West."

"Prostitution as a force for civilization? Who would buy that?"

"You're the politician. You spin the story. Give a little speech to the audience. Break it to them easy. Just don't kill the new pageant."

"You're making my head hurt."

"That's not me. That's too many Tecates and Autumn."

He returned his brother's gaze. *Autumn.* God, he missed her.

"Straighten things out. You need that woman."

"How? I haven't been myself since she walked into town hall. I've let things slide. I've—"

"Things got done, Mike. You know that Evelyn, all on her own, sent out the economic development kits to the mailing list we purchased."

"Hell, I forgot all about that."

"You've been, uh, busy. That's the point. Evelyn handled it. You don't have to hold my hand. Or the town's. We'll figure it out. Live your life, Mike. Let someone else watch out for you for a change. Evelyn. Me. And Autumn."

"That's over." He shook his head. "She thinks I'm an uptight ass. Maybe I am. I hate that she's a stripper. I hate men staring at her, seeing her naked, wanting her. How do you handle it?"

Mark smiled. "Jasmine loves the revue. She wasn't so comfortable with straight stripping, but burlesque has more artistry to it and she likes that. I try not to think too hard about it. But you can be sure if it ever drags her down, makes her hurt inside, I'll help her stop. I'm there for her however she needs me."

"Yeah. I see that." In fact, that was how he felt, too. Autumn *wanted* to quit stripping. But when he'd pointed it out, she'd wanted to tee-up on his skull.

"You can fix it, Mike," Mark said. "Start with the pageant. Show her you're not a tight ass all the time."

"I'll think about it."

"I'm right. I know I am."

"I said I'd think about it."

"One more thing I need to tell you. I know I said I'd hold off, but there's a guy from Tucson who wants to buy Fields Real Estate. The timing's right."

"You're selling?"

Mark nodded. "I found a Phoenix agency where I can start right away. I won't leave you or the town in the lurch." He rattled off whom he would ask to take over the chamber and the economic development committee, offering to consult by phone and return frequently, to help with the transition.

Mike just listened, sadness climbing in him. His brother was leaving home. He was unreasonably sad about it.

"I know you think this is too fast," Mark said. "We could do the long distance thing, but my gut tells me I need to be there for Jasmine and Sabrina. I don't want to miss another day as a family." He stopped, waiting for Mike's response.

In the past, he might have made one more argument,

but he could see now that Mark was different, more confident. He sat with his shoulders back, his eyes steady, not jumpy, not expecting criticism. The man knew what he was doing. He had a plan and he was implementing it.

It all came clear, like rain swiped from a blurred windshield. He'd been seeing his brother wrong. He had to fix it. "Let me know how I can help you."

Mark looked a little startled. "Great. I appreciate that." He paused, then leaned over to give Mike a brusque hug. "Thanks for hearing me out."

"You're my brother. It's my job."

"I'll get you that history to read. And let me know how I can help you, okay?"

Mike took the printout Mark gave him back to his room and flopped onto his bed to read for a few minutes before he had to get ready for the final festival meeting.

What would he say to Autumn when he saw her? His lids burned from the hangover and he let them drop down for a second of rest.

MIKE AWOKE WITH A JERK and stared at the clock. 10:00 a.m. The meeting started at nine and he hadn't even finalized the agenda. Shit. He called town hall and got the machine. Where was Evelyn? Off somewhere knitting something, no doubt.

He threw on his clothes and raced into town. The building seemed deserted at first, but he heard the hum of voices and headed down the hall. Through the conference room window, he saw the meeting was in progress. Evelyn and Autumn sat at the head of the table. Autumn was speaking to the group.

Evelyn spotted him and stepped out. "We're on the

committee reports now. I did the agenda and Autumn's running the meeting."

"You did the agenda?" he repeated stupidly.

"I figured out your notes. I don't wear Nikes for nothing." She bounced back and forth. "Balls of my feet."

"And Autumn's running the meeting?" Another stupid repetition.

"It's not that tough, hon. You gotta learn to hand off the baton." Great. More advice. And this from Evelyn, who'd suddenly developed a work ethic.

He reached to open the door, but she caught his arm. "Wait. I'm saying this with love, Mike, but do not go in there and act like we've all been waiting for you to start the *real* meeting."

"Okay. I get it. I'll behave."

"And you look as awful as Autumn. What happened? Never mind, just apologize to her. Right or wrong, it's good for the soul. Don't blow this. She's the best thing that's happened to you since…since…I don't know…puberty. Just fix it." Evelyn opened the door and waved him in front of her.

He took the empty chair at the foot of the long table, facing Autumn.

She stopped talking. "We're on agenda item five, Mayor, if you'd like to take over."

Eyes ping-ponged from her to him and back.

"I'm sorry I'm late," he said. "You're doing fine. I'll jump in when I have something to add."

"Great," she said, faltering for a second—her eyes looked so sad—then she asked Celia to continue.

The meeting went fine. Maybe not as orderly as he liked and Autumn allowed the speakers to ramble, but every topic got covered just fine.

Maybe he *had* done too much for the town. Maybe he could move to Phoenix and pass out flyers for the strip club.

"Mayor Mike?"

"Huh?" He realized Autumn had called his name more than once. "Sorry."

"I asked if you thought we'd missed anything?"

"Not that I know of, except to mention that I'll be discussing with the pageant director some changes in light of new historical information."

Around the room there were puzzled looks.

"You will?" Autumn asked.

"I will," he said. He wasn't giving up this time. Autumn said she always took the easy road, but he'd begun to see he did that all the time, too. He'd been too quick to give up what he wanted, blaming it on duty to his family or responsibility for the town. Now he wanted Autumn in his life. He wasn't giving up. He would show her. And he would start with the pageant.

It was Wednesday night, two days before the Founder's Day festival and Autumn sat at the table at Louie's, nervously running her palm over the linen cloth. Jasmine had set up the dinner for her, Mark and Sabrina, who'd finished camp, and invited Autumn and Mike to join them.

The Monday after the festival they would all head to Phoenix, so this was a celebration of the end of the summer adventure and the beginning of a new life for Jasmine, Mark and Sabrina. It would be the last dinner with Mike, too.

Mike. Just thinking his name made her start to shake. Why was she so nervous? They'd worked together fine, finalizing the details of the festival, too busy to argue or share looks of regret. They'd even bowled together, ending up in fourth place. Not bad, except that there were only six teams in the league.

Maybe this didn't have to be goodbye. Jasmine had told her Mike had relented on the new pageant, though they'd made the dance G-rated, added fabric to the costumes and Mike would make some kind of introductory speech. She'd agreed to dance.

For now, she was so nervous she could hardly see straight. The lovely smells of garlic and tomato filled her nose, but her appetite was lost to her. What would she say to the man?

"Hey there."

She jerked her head to find Mike smiling down at her, his eyes full of the familiar heat.

"Black lace bra. Matching thong," she said. The old joke burst out automatically.

"You make it tough to sit," he murmured, lowering himself into the chair beside her, dangerously handsome in a dark silk shirt and dress jeans. He put his arm on the back of her chair and leaned close to her ear to whisper, "Plaid boxers."

"The ones with the raveled hem?" Her heart stopped.

"The ones you ripped with your teeth? Yep."

"Mmm. Sorry."

"I wasn't."

Arousal hummed through her, as predictable as sunshine on an Arizona day. "You cut yourself." She touched the dot of blood on his jaw.

"I'm shaky, I guess. Not sleeping well."

"Festival stress?"

"Uh-uh. I miss you." He leaned closer. He had dark hollows under his eyes and his smile crinkles seemed fainter than they should be.

"Me, too." She spent many sleepless hours under the stars, swinging in the hammock her neighbor Winnie had loaned her, wishing for what couldn't be, wondering how much of what Jasmine had said about her was correct. Was she too negative? Could happiness just fall into her lap?

Even Barbara's herbal sleep remedy hadn't helped, though the woman's grumpy friendship had been a comfort.

Now Autumn looked into Mike's chocolate eyes and fought the urge to lean in for a kiss. Luckily, before she did anything foolish, the waiter appeared and they ordered a bottle of wine, four glasses, and a diet Shirley Temple for Sabrina.

Celia and Dan walked up to them. "Good job on the tournament, you two," Celia said.

"It was fun," Autumn said.

"Fourth place is great."

"Except there were only six teams," she added.

"Well, there's that… You need to come in for those highlights."

Autumn fingered her hair, which she'd worn loose. She wore it loose every day now. She'd realized that what she wore or how she looked wasn't nearly as important as what she knew and could do. "Thanks, anyway. I'm headed home Monday."

"So soon? I'm sorry to hear that." Celia bit her lip. "Listen, I want you to know that the girls meant no harm the other day. Raylene's daughter got into a drug mess, so it eases her pain to drum up other people's problems."

"It doesn't matter." Autumn shrugged.

"Sure it does. I'm gonna have Evelyn stitch me a sampler—If You Can't Say Something Nice, Go Gargle Something Sour."

Autumn laughed. The incident seemed so far away now.

"Your friend Jasmine is a hoot. I was touching up her extensions and she told me in Phoenix you can take classes in pole-dancing for *exercise*. I'd love to get that going around here. I wish she and Mark weren't leaving." She turned to Mike. "You must be fit to be tied about that."

"The man knows what he's doing."

Autumn was surprised to hear Mike say that.

"I know, but we'll miss him, won't we, Mike?" Celia patted his arm in sympathy.

"Yeah. And I was just getting to know him." Mike gave a wry smile. "Amazing what you can learn about people when you actually listen to them."

"You'll just have to visit Phoenix more," Celia said. "Which you'll want to, I'm sure, when you hear Heidi's news."

"What news?"

"I'll let her tell you." She winked. "Not every stylist is a gossip, you know." She nodded at Autumn. "Try to find a few minutes before you go for me to do those highlights now."

"I'll try. Thanks." She smiled at Celia, who was obviously trying to make it up to her for the gossip. Gossip was human, she guessed. And, meanwhile, Celia was wishing for pole-dancing classes in town. That was pretty open-minded. Maybe when you knew people, let them know you, things worked out better. Maybe that was how you fit in....

"I bet Heidi's pregnant," Mike mused to Autumn when Celia and Dan had moved on.

"That would be great." She smiled at him, feeling a clutch when she remembered their conversation about having kids. They'd been so carried away.

"My sister's something else. I'll always be grateful to her for sending you to me. That was the best decision I made in a long time."

"I enjoyed the job. I learned a lot."

"You did great, Autumn. Nothing that's happened changed that." He picked up his wineglass, then winced.

"What's wrong?"

He held out his palm, which showed the remains of blisters.

"Too much golf?"

He nodded.

"Are you sorry it happened, Mike?"

"Not a bit. I'm sorry we ended it." He took her hand between both of his, careful of the sore one. "I've been doing some thinking, Autumn...."

"You have?" Her heart climbed into her throat, but before either of them could say more, tan arms wrapped around her neck and squeezed. "Surprise!" Sabrina pressed her cheek against Autumn's.

Mike withdrew his hands and smiled, holding her gaze, telling her they would talk more later.

Autumn closed her eyes and held on to Sabrina, overwhelmed with love for her. These weeks with Mike had made her more vulnerable to her emotions. Her safe face seemed far away.

"See how tanned I got?" Sabrina said, holding out an arm. "And check this out." She made a muscle. "Canoeing did that."

"You look terrific," Autumn said. She'd slimmed down, too, which had to help her body image. "That's a diet Shirley Temple for you."

Sabrina took a gulp. "Mmm. Delish."

Mark and Jasmine sat down and they exchanged greetings. Mike poured them wine.

"Look what Mark made me." Sabrina held out a handbag made of different colors of plastic strips. "He's buying his way into my heart. Isn't that hot?"

Mark beamed.

"I told Mark to trust his love," Jasmine said, "but he just ignored me." She kissed Mark on the mouth.

Sabrina groaned. "They're all the time so disgusting and mushy. *Honey* this and *sugar* that. You get fat just listening."

"I don't know why two people in love make you squirm," Jasmine said.

"We're happy for them, aren't we, Sabbie?" Autumn said, catching Mike's smile.

"I guess." Sabrina grabbed a menu.

It was quiet while everyone studied the selections, until Sabrina announced, "I want the surf and turf."

"That's too much food, Sabbie," Jasmine said. "Why don't you try the kiddie menu?"

"Because I'm not a kiddie."

"She can order what she wants, sweetheart," Mark said. "It's on me tonight. No worries."

"We have a budget and she knows it, Mark." Jasmine's voice had an edge.

"But he said he's buying," Sabrina said.

"Mark's being polite. You will not take advantage."

"Let's not make a scene, Jas," Mark said, a little paternally.

"I'm not making a scene," she replied, too loudly. "I'm being a parent. Never having been one, you don't understand that."

Ouch. Autumn cringed. Mark looked stung.

"I want surf and turf," Sabrina whined.

Tension beat the air with angry wings. Autumn and Mike ducked their noses into their goblets.

"It's surf *or* turf, not both," Jasmine said firmly. "If you're still hungry after that, we'll order the other one."

"That's not fair. I haven't been in a restaurant in a month. I should get what I want."

"What your mother says goes," Mark said, taking Jasmine's hand. "She's the parent." He turned to Jasmine, clearly asking her forgiveness. Jasmine nodded, giving it.

"I could still not like you, you know," Sabrina threatened, but the energy was fading from her words.

"I was thinking of making a backpack next. Out of duct tape, maybe?" Mark said.

The adults chuckled and Sabrina had to fight not to smile.

Autumn was impressed by how that had gone. Jasmine had been calm and self-assured. Mark had backed off when he was out of line. They were acting like decent parents, not lust-crazed lovers.

Mike shot her a look that told her he'd noticed, too, then lifted his glass. "How about a toast? To Mark and Jasmine and Sabrina. May you have all the duct tape you need."

They clicked glasses.

"And to Mike," Mark said, lifting his glass, abruptly serious. "I couldn't want a better brother."

"Oh, yeah, you could," Mike said. "But you're stuck

with me." Mike cleared his throat to hide his emotion. "And ditto." Everyone got busy drinking wine.

"Same for you, Autumn," Jasmine said, lunging across the table for a rough hug. This time, Autumn managed not to bite her tongue. "Even when you tell me I can't afford Jimmy Choo's on final clearance."

"I'm happy for you, Jas," she said when Jasmine sat back down. Everyone looked around the table and Autumn realized this was how a family felt—full of trust, warmth, constancy. Time and miles and choices might come between them, but the bond would remain.

They ordered dinner and started eating. Autumn's gaze fell often on Mark and Jasmine. She caught Mike doing the same thing. Neither she nor Mike had given the pair the benefit of the doubt.

"Ahem." Sabrina elbowed Autumn in the middle of staring at the couple. "Haven't you ever seen two people in love before?"

Autumn grinned. "Not close up, I guess."

"It's kinda cool. Until they start with the tongues. *That* is way gross."

"Oh, absolutely," Autumn said, giving an eye roll for old times' sake.

"Disgusting." Mike winked at her.

God, how she missed him. She wanted another chance. They'd both been thinking, right? Maybe they could figure out how to keep this vacation going a little longer. Maybe it was time to let her heart lead. Maybe Esmie's psychic vibe was right after all.

16

AUTUMN WAS SO BUSY handling last-minute details on the first day of the festival, she didn't see much of Friday's activities, barely catching a glimpse of the parade out the window as it went by. She made the pageant rehearsal that night. The simplified dance number was easy to master and it was fun to be part of a production again. It almost made up for the high school fiasco.

On Saturday, she managed to enjoy some of the events: the picnic, the dedication of the welcome sign, the desert foods cook-off—Barbara's salsa took first place—and the picnic games, including the strangest one she'd ever seen. Cow-pie tic-tac-toe, which Evelyn's granddaughter Kimmie won. The silent auction raised eight thousand dollars for the Children's Fund.

As the day passed, she was surprised how many people knew her and spoke to her—her neighbors, of course, and most of the town employees, the bowling league players and all the festival committee chairs.

She was nibbling on a prickly pear jelly candy from the Cactus Confections booth, ready to head to the final rehearsal, when she noticed Mike talking to Raylene, the woman from the beauty parlor who had the druggie daughter.

She and Mike had been so busy they'd barely spoken all day. Mike was constantly on the run—dealing with parking snafus, making announcements, shaking hands, officiating at the cook-off, playing his role of town father with relish.

He was also fired up because Wayne Whittaker was making an offer on the Desert Paradise. Mike warned her it was no guarantee, but she could see how proud he was that he'd achieved this for the town. She was proud, too, that she'd started the ball rolling.

She wanted to tell him she was heading off for rehearsal, so she approached the pair. Mike had braced a huge bag of pre-wrapped cotton candy against a table, evidently headed to the town's snack booth when Raylene must have stopped him.

"I just told her that our mayor would never allow a strip show on our stage," Raylene was saying when Autumn got close.

"It will be dancing, Raylene. No disrobing at all and the show is G-rated. You'll enjoy it." He caught Autumn's eye and smiled. "Hey there," he said softly.

"But you're allowing a stripper to perform in our pageant?" Raylene repeated, sounding scandalized.

"She's a great dancer, isn't she, Autumn?"

"Excellent," she said to Raylene. "And a terrific costume designer. She did all the costumes herself."

"In fact, you might want to go up to Phoenix and check out her burlesque revue. It's like a Vegas show, right, Autumn? Maybe you could tell Raylene more about it, set her straight."

Tell her off, if you want. Give her what for. That's what he was saying. But looking at the woman, thinking of what an unhappy person she had to be to be so overwrought over this, Autumn only said, "We get a lot of couples, Raylene. It's tasteful and creative and fun. We've had great reviews."

"We? Are you saying…?"

"That I'm in the revue? Yep."

"But I thought you worked at town hall."

"Autumn is a woman of many talents." Mike looked at her, his affection laced with heat.

"Thank you." The knot in her throat made it hard to speak.

"In fact," Mike said, still watching her, "maybe we could talk you into bringing the show down to Copper Corners as a fund-raiser? Think of all the money we could make for the Children's Fund. Right, Raylene?"

"For the Children's Fund? I don't think that would be… That wouldn't be…"

"Think about it. I've got to get this cotton candy into the molars of our children." He lifted the pastel rainbow of fluffy sugar, winked at Autumn, then strode away from the slack-jawed Raylene. He looked so confident and strong. She remembered when she first saw him how that struck her, how he looked as though he got his way without trying very hard. Except she knew now that he'd turned away from things he wanted in favor of duty and responsibility. She could help him with that. She wanted to.

She turned to Raylene. "You need to lighten up. Everything's not black and white, good or bad. That's what makes things interesting."

She hurried after Mike, catching him at the refreshment booth, where he was handing over his sugary burden. "I can't believe you said that to Raylene."

"Shocked the hell out of her, too." He shrugged, a

mischievous twinkle in his eyes. He leaned in and spoke low. "I told you I don't care what people think. Strip if you want to or quit. It's up to you. Just be honest with yourself about what you want." He touched her cheek. "I'm not quitting on you, Autumn."

"Mike…I…"

"Let's talk, okay?"

"Okay. Except now I have rehearsal and—"

"And there's a sound problem on the karaoke stage and the cow-pie clean-up crew is MIA. So let's make it after the pageant tonight."

She was still nodding when he walked away. It was clear to her now. Mike was not the one with a problem with her career. Jasmine had been right about that, too.

Autumn was finished stripping. The idea of it made her feel empty inside. She'd hidden that for years behind her game face. Being with Mike brought everything front and center. She couldn't hide it any more.

Just as she no longer needed a sexy costume under her business suit to feel confident in her new career, she didn't need to hide from Mike behind being a stripper.

Don't disappear on me. Mike had insisted on seeing all of her—body and mind and soul—and she'd try to hide from his love, from the risk of giving her heart to him. She was picking up her heart from the curb and dusting it right off.

Oh, yeah. They had a lot to talk about.

IT WAS ALMOST CURTAIN TIME and everyone was bustling around arranging props, adjusting costumes, finalizing makeup. Hardly able to breathe in her bustier, Autumn peeked through the curtains at the restless crowd of

Copper Corners families who filled the auditorium to overflowing.

It was fun to be part of the excitement, enjoying the nervous laughter of the cast, the smells, the bright lights, the anticipation of the crowd's pleasure. She felt it all. She didn't need to hide from a single feeling. She was right there, all there, fully present behind her eyes.

And full of hope. So strange. She felt fresh and new, as if she were seeing the world and the people in it for the first time.

"Big crowd?" Mike's voice in her ear sent warmth flooding through her.

"Looks like the whole town." She turned and smiled at him. He looked great in his period costume—dark suit, bowler hat, embroidered vest, even a watch chain—but he was very pale. "Are you nervous?"

"I don't know why. I speak in public all the time. Maybe because this is a play and I'm in costume. I'm not much of an actor." He shrugged.

"Just picture them naked," she said.

"I'd rather picture you that way."

Heat rushed through her so fast her knees gave out.

"You okay?" He caught her by the arms.

"Barely," she said. "After that."

He grinned. "Do me a favor and don't tell me what you've got on under that." His gaze swept her costume. "Wouldn't look good for the mayor to limp on stage with a bulge."

"But you love a challenge. Black open bra, tiger-striped thong," she murmured.

A shudder passed through him. "You're a cruel woman, Autumn Beshkin."

"You love it."

"I do," he said with a sigh. "God help me, I do." He looked down at her with such a charming blend of adoration and agony she wanted to laugh and dance and sing and cry all at once.

"Places!" Sheila shouted, clapping her hands.

"Wish me luck," Mike said, patting his top hat and tugging at his vest.

"Break a leg," she whispered, adjusting his bow tie.

"No way. I'm not breaking anything that will keep me from chasing you down later."

She laughed. "You'll do great. You were born to give speeches." Mike left and she joined Jasmine offstage.

"Feels good to perform again, doesn't it?" Jasmine whispered, her feathered hat vibrating with excitement. "I miss the revue so much."

Autumn only smiled. She hoped Nevada and Jasmine would understand her need to leave, to concentrate on school. She would help them audition and train her replacement, but she wouldn't dance another season.

"You work things out with Mike?" Jasmine asked.

"We're going to talk."

"Think of the glass as half full. Sure, Mike is bossy and boring and—"

"Hey, he's not that bad."

"But he's also loving and generous and sweet and funny. Glass half full, see?"

"I do." She studied her friend. "I also see that you've been way more on top of things than I gave you credit for."

"Hey, you helped me get there. And you hardly ever roll your eyes at me."

"Only when you're not looking."

Jasmine laughed. "I need your sarcasm. It gives my life spice."

They grinned at each other for a few seconds. Then Sheila cued Mike and he stepped out onto the stage. There was loud applause, whistles and shouts. The town loved its mayor, no matter how overbearing and paternal he might be.

And she loved him, too. She couldn't handle just listening off stage, so she tiptoed down the stairs so that she could see him, without the audience seeing her in the dark. He was golden under the white theater lights, noble and proud, handsome in his old-fashioned suit, accepting the applause of the townspeople he loved so much.

She fingered the lace Jasmine had added to the costume neckline for modesty. Autumn didn't mind that or the scaled-back dance. Her anger had been a smokescreen for her doubts about her own respectability. She knew Mike's speech held a message for her, too.

First, he welcomed everyone to the pageant and thanked each person by name who'd worked on it. Then he introduced the descendents of the town founder, sitting in the front row wearing flowers, and paused for applause.

She watched him take a deep breath before he began.

"We all know that history is in the eye of the beholder. And the beholder interprets what he sees as he sees fit. For example, the story of Copper Corners as a mining town could be a tale of blood-thirsty greed and lawless avarice. Or it could be about adventure and courage and fresh starts.

"I don't know about you, but I prefer the good

version. And when I tell you the surprising facts the talented creators of this pageant discovered about our history, I hope you'll share my interpretation."

He paused to let his words sink in. The crowd murmured.

"The story you're about to see could be a tale of scandal. Or it could be about love and sacrifice and building a community."

The crowd muttered and he waited, making eye contact here and there. He caught Autumn's eye. She tried to encourage him and she watched him visibly relax. Was he picturing her naked? Or the crowd?

"You see, it seems that the oldest building in town, where Cactus Confections now stands, was not a community hall per se. It was a bordello called Arizona Rose's Desert Palace."

He waited while the crowd gasped and buzzed in reaction.

"It seems that a famous Chicago madam came to the Territory to investigate a mining claim she'd inherited. While here, she fell in love with miner Josiah Bremmer, our town founder. Unable to leave him, she changed her name to Arizona Rose and opened a new establishment near the Copper Strike Mine. Our town grew around that business. The Common Bread Colony soon followed and the history we all know followed from there."

He let the words sink in, waited for the noise to settle.

"Scandalous, correct? Not necessarily. Let me tell you more about Arizona Rose. She was a civilizing force in the town. She made the miners write home regularly, urged them to bring their families out West. She talked one of them into becoming a sheriff—a dangerous job for the day.

"She organized a school and made sure her girls learned to read. She raised money to care for orphans. Arizona Rose was a feminist of her day, speaking out for women's suffrage, leading by example, working to build the community. Not so scandalous in my mind. Honorable. Courageous. Wise." He paused again. This time the crowd was silent. You could hear a pin drop in the room. Autumn hunted the faces, looking for disapproval, shock, anger. Everyone seemed to be holding their breath.

"It was a different time," Mike continued. "A rougher time, but some things are timeless—the love of a man and a woman for each other, the love of home and land, the desire to make our town something we can all be proud of. And that love, that mission, lives on today in all we do, from the purchase of Desert Paradise by Mr. Wayne Whittaker." He paused for startled applause. "To Ned Langton, who'll be taking over the Chamber for my brother Mark, who has passed the baton so he can move to Phoenix with the woman he loves, to how we celebrate the good times and stand by each other in the bad ones."

Applause started slowly and built. There were whistles and a few shouts of approval.

"I love my town. And I love the people in it, with their warts and weaknesses, their virtue and courage, their stubborn streaks and their hearts full of love." He looked straight at Autumn.

She smiled at him. He was right. Warts and virtues, weakness and courage existed in everyone, small town or big city. In herself and Mike, in her mother and her brothers, in Barbara and Evelyn and even Raylene, who had a way to go to earn Autumn's respect. You stuck with it. You didn't quit.

"I know Chicago Rose grew to love this town, too, as much as she loved Josiah," Mike continued. "So, hold your love of our town in your heart as you watch this story. I proudly invite you to enjoy *Copper Corners—The Town That Love Built.*"

The applause this time was uproarious and Autumn laughed out loud in relief and pleasure. She was proud of Mike and how he'd given the new pageant dignity and honor. It was all in how you looked at it, like so many things.

The pageant began and the time flew, the details blurring around her. The production wouldn't win any awards, by any means. Jasmine was stiff and missed some lines. The covered wagon lost a wheel. And, without the sexy energy, the dance number came off short and a little dull.

None of that mattered to Autumn. Or anybody in the auditorium. The performers had a blast and it showed and the applause went on and on. There were three curtain calls.

THE SUN WAS SETTING when Mike finally caught up with Autumn at the Ferris wheel, on the golf course where their affair had begun. He'd suggested the spot.

He handed over the required eight coupons to the carnie in charge, and helped her into the car he'd insisted on—number seven, the one they'd made love in.

He put his arm around her, grateful beyond words for the pleasure of her body nestled into his. At first they just sat there, breathing slowly, feeling how it was to touch each other again, climbing through the dry desert air, then sinking down to the smells of funnel cake, dust, machine oil and metal, and, beneath it all, the desert itself.

Mike looked out over the crowd—his town—and felt the usual sense of belonging, the urge to do right by the place. Then he looked at Autumn and felt something new—love, commitment, a sense of deep purpose and fresh hope for the future.

He had to have her with him. Whatever it took, even if he had to leave this town he loved so much, he wasn't giving up. All his life he'd taken the easy road, done what was expected, not always what he truly wanted.

"This is nice, isn't it?" she said, looking up at him.

"Now that I have you, yeah." He shifted in the seat so he could look into her face, pink from the day in the sun, her dark eyes glowing in the dusk light.

"I need you in my life, Autumn. If you want me in Phoenix handing out flyers for your show, I'll do that. I'll support you however you need me to."

Her lips quivered as she smiled, showing him his words had touched her. "I'm finished being a stripper, Mike. I hung on to the idea because I was afraid about the future and I was defensive about it. I guess I felt a little ashamed."

"I love you no matter what you are—a stripper, an accountant, a grant writer, a crossing guard. I'll defend you to anyone who dares to criticize you."

His loyalty warmed her.

He cupped her cheeks. "You make me feel the way I felt before my folks died—like the world is a safe place. Of course things go wrong, but with you in my arms, I don't have to hold on to everything else so damn tight." He swallowed, clenching his jaw against welling emotion.

Autumn's eyes shimmered with tears. One fell to her cheek and she left it there. He was glad.

"I love that you had me so wild I made love to you in a bowling alley," he continued, "and on this golf course, and in this." He patted the steel bar that crossed their waists.

"Maybe we're just in lust," she said, biting her lip, her eyes a little scared. "Like Mark and Jasmine."

"We should be so lucky," he said.

"You're right. We were wrong about them."

"We assumed the worst. Not fair. They know what they're doing."

They reached the ground and the carnie leaned over to release them. Mike fished out a twenty. "We'll let you know when we're done," he said, handing it to him.

The guy smiled a gap-toothed grin and stepped back. The wheel pulled them up in the air again.

"So, we know what we're doing, you think?" Autumn said, hope brimming in her eyes.

He would have to show her. He kissed her and kept kissing her through all the doubts. Just like that first night when their connection had opened his mind to everything he'd wanted but let pass by.

It was the applause that brought Autumn to her senses. She broke off the kiss and looked down at the sea of faces grinning up at them, applauding, whistling and shouting approval.

"The woman I love," Mike yelled down to the crowd, who responded with a great cheer.

"Mrs. Mayor, if you'll have me," he said softly to her.

"Let's not get ahead of ourselves," she said, but she felt the lightning strike of sureness to her core. She could make a life with this man. "I love you and I want to be with you. That's what I know so far."

She'd been about to pull her old trick and quit before she got what she wanted. She finally had the confidence she needed to go all the way. "You make me want to fit in, Mike. For the first time in my life."

"I'm glad to hear that. So how do we do this? Copper Corners is a small town. There's not much to do but bowl and gossip."

"But people care about each other. They work out their problems. They don't take a cab out of town."

"What about school?" Mike asked.

"The U of A has a program and my credits will transfer. I can commute."

"And work?"

"Lydia wants to extend her leave. And maybe I could be that grant writer for a while. I found a historic preservation grant and it needs an administrator." She wasn't sure how they would manage all that. For now, she was taking Esmeralda's advice and leading with her heart, which was nowhere near the curb and never would be again. She couldn't wait to tell Esmie.

"I'm afraid you'll be bored. I mean, your underwear alone will keep me enthralled for years, but you have higher entertainment standards."

She laughed and kissed him. "Tucson's not far. And Celia wants pole-dancing classes. That'll be fun."

"Oh, yeah. We'll give Raylene a gift certificate."

"There you go." She laughed. "Maybe when I finish with school and you finish being mayor, we can move to Phoenix? I want my own business one day. When I'm ready." There would be time to see how she wanted to use her degree. There were suddenly other things that mattered, too. A life with Mike. Maybe a family?

So many possibilities she'd never allowed herself to consider. She hadn't dared to hope.

"All I need is you, Autumn. To remind me to have a life, to go on vacation, to—"

"To take a sex break?" she added. "Say, in the town hall bathroom?"

"As long as we don't break Evelyn's ceramics."

"Maybe just the ugly ones." She laughed. "I think we'll be fine." She had faith, a new and startling condition she hoped to hang on to forever.

"Maybe one day you'll run for mayor, Autumn."

"Copper Corners with a stripper as mayor?" She laughed. "Who knows? Maybe love does make all things possible."

Right now, glowing with Mike's love, she felt as if she could conquer the world. Not because of how he saw her, but because of how she'd begun to see herself.

Mike kissed her again and she melted into it. Here was love and support and passion, and so much more.

Glass half empty? How about filled to the brim and spilling over? And she would feel that way for a very long time. At least until the end of the ride.

And Mike had plenty of twenties.

* * * * *

Don't miss the conclusion of the
DOING IT…BETTER! *miniseries*
Be sure to pick up
AT HIS FINGERTIPS
by Dawn Atkins
Coming in April 2007 from Harlequin Blaze

Happily ever after is just the beginning...

Turn the page for a sneak preview of
A HEARTBEAT AWAY
by Eleanor Jones

Harlequin Everlasting—
Every great love has a story to tell. ™
A brand-new series from Harlequin Books

Special? A prickle ran down my neck and my heart started to beat in my ears. Was today really special?

"Tuck in," he ordered.

I turned my attention to the feast that he had spread out on the ground. Thick, home-cooked-ham sandwiches, sausage rolls fresh from the oven and a huge variety of mouthwatering scones and pastries. Hunger pangs took over, and I closed my eyes and bit into soft homemade bread.

When we were finally finished, I lay back against the bluebells with a groan, clutching my stomach.

Daniel laughed. "Your eyes are bigger than your stomach," he told me.

I leaned across to deliver a punch to his arm, but he rolled away, and when my fist met fresh air I collapsed in a fit of giggles before relaxing on my back and staring up into the flawless blue sky. We lay like that for quite a while, Daniel and I, side by side in companionable silence, until he stretched out his hand in an arc that encompassed the whole area.

"Don't you think that this is the most beautiful place in the entire world?"

His voice held a passion that echoed my own feelings, and I rose onto my elbow and picked a buttercup to hide the emotion that clogged my throat.

"Roll over onto your back," I urged, prodding him with my forefinger. He obliged with a broad grin, and I reached across to place the yellow flower beneath his chin.

"Now, let us see if you like butter."

When a yellow light shone on the tanned skin below his jaw, I laughed.

"There…you do."

For an instant our eyes met, and I had the strangest sense that I was drowning in those honey-brown depths. The scent of bluebells engulfed me. A roaring filled my ears, and then, unexpectedly, in one smooth movement Daniel rolled me onto my back and plucked a buttercup of his own.

"And do *you* like butter, Lucy McTavish?" he asked. When he placed the flower against my skin, time stood still.

His long lean body was suspended over mine, pinning me against the grass. Daniel…dear, comfortable, familiar Daniel was suddenly bringing out in me the strangest sensations.

"Do you, Lucy McTavish?" he asked again, his voice low and vibrant.

My eyes flickered toward his, the whisper of a sigh escaped my lips and although a strange lethargy had crept into my limbs, I somehow felt as if all my nerve endings were on fire. He felt it, too—I could see it in his warm brown eyes. And when he lowered his face to mine, it seemed to me the most natural thing in the world.

None of the kisses I had ever experienced could have even begun to prepare me for the feel of Daniel's lips on mine. My entire body floated on a tide of ecstasy that shut out everything but his soft, warm mouth, and I knew that this was what I had been waiting for the whole of my life.

"Oh, Lucy." He pulled away to look into my eyes. "Why haven't we done this before?"

Holding his gaze, I gently touched his cheek, then I curled my fingers through the short thick hair at the base of his skull, overwhelmed by the longing to drown again in the sensations that flooded our bodies. And when his long tanned fingers crept across my tingling skin, I knew I could deny him nothing.

* * * * *

Be sure to look for
A HEARTBEAT AWAY,
available February 27, 2007.
And look, too, for
THE DEPTH OF LOVE by Margot Early,
the story of a couple who must learn that
love comes in many guises—and in the end
it's the only thing that counts.

EVERLASTING LOVE™

Every great love has a story to tell™

Save $1.⁰⁰ off

the purchase of
any Harlequin
Everlasting Love novel

Coupon valid from January 1, 2007
until April 30, 2007.

**Valid at retail outlets in the U.S. only.
Limit one coupon per customer.**

RETAILER: Harlequin Enterprises Limited will pay the face value of this coupon plus
8¢ if submitted by the customer for this product only. Any other use constitutes fraud.
Coupon is nonassignable. Void if taxed, prohibited or restricted by law. Consumer
must pay any government taxes. Void if copied. For reimbursement submit coupons
and proof of sales directly to: Harlequin Enterprises Ltd., P.O. Box 880478, El Paso,
TX 88588-0478, U.S.A. Cash value 1/100¢. Valid in the U.S. only. ® is a trademark of
Harlequin Enterprises Ltd. Trademarks marked with ® are registered in the United
States and/or other countries.

5 65373 00076 2   (8100) 0 11302

HEUSCPN0407

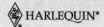

HARLEQUIN®

EVERLASTING LOVE™

Every great love has a story to tell™

Save $1.00 off

the purchase of
any Harlequin
Everlasting Love novel

Coupon valid from January 1, 2007
until April 30, 2007.

Valid at retail outlets in Canada only.
Limit one coupon per customer.

52607370

HECDNCPN0407

REQUEST YOUR FREE BOOKS!

2 FREE NOVELS PLUS 2 FREE GIFTS!

♦ HARLEQUIN®

Blaze®

Red-hot reads!

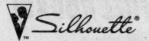

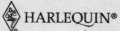

HARLEQUIN®

Blaze™

COMING NEXT MONTH

#309 BEYOND DARING Kathleen O'Reilly
The Red Choo Diaries, Bk. 2
Hot and handsome Jeff Brooks has his hands full "babysitting" his P.R. agency's latest wild-child client, Sheldon Summerville. When she crosses the line, he has no choice but to follow....

#310 A BREATH AWAY Wendy Etherington
The Wrong Bed
Security expert Jade Broussard has one simple rule—never sleep with clients. So why is her latest client, Remy Tremaine, in her bed, sliding his delicious hands all over her? Whatever the reason, she'll toss him out…as soon as she's had enough of those hands!

#311 JUST ONE LOOK Joanne Rock
Night Eyes, Bk. 2
Watching the woman he's supposed to protect take off her clothes is throwing NYPD ballistics expert Warren Vitalis off his game. Instead of focusing on the case at hand, all he can think about is getting Tabitha Everheart's naked self into his bed!

#312 SLOW HAND LUKE Debbi Rawlins
Champion rodeo cowboy Luke McCall claims he's wrongly accused, so he's hiding out. But at a cop's place? Annie Corrigan is one suspicious sergeant, yet has her own secrets. Too bad her wild attraction to her houseguest isn't one of them…

#313 RECKONING Jo Leigh
In Too Deep…, Bk. 3
Delta Force soldier Nate Pratchett is on a mission. He's protecting sexy scientist Tamara Jones while hunting down the bad guys. But sleeping with the vulnerable Tam is distracting him big-time. Especially since he's started battling feelings of love…

#314 TAKE ON ME Sarah Mayberry
Secret Lives of Daytime Divas, Bk. 1
How can Sadie Post be Dylan Anderson's boss when she can't forget the humiliation he caused her on prom night? Worse, her lustful teenage longings for him haven't exactly gone away. There's only one resolution: seduce the man until she's feeling better. *Much* better.

www.eHarlequin.com